War

In memory of Donald Lush (1935-45)

First published in Great Britain in 2010 and in the USA in 2011 by
Frances Lincoln Children's Books, 4 Torriano Mews,
Torriano Avenue, London NW5 2RZ
www.franceslincoln.com

A catalogue record of this book is available from the British Library.

ISBN: 978-1-84780-054-1

Set in Palatino

Printed in Croydon, Surrey, UK by CPI Bookmarque Ltd. in June 2010

1 3 5 7 9 8 6 4 2

Ronnie's War

Bernard Ashley

F

FRANCES LINCOLN
CHILDREN'S BOOKS

Contents

Blitzkrieg

Chapter One

'Don't you dare talk to me like that! You'd change your tune if your dad was here!'

Ronnie felt a great lump in his throat. He shouldn't have said what he did.

'I didn't mean *you*, I meant her. *Her.*'

'That's still not something you call a lady. Your father would wash your mouth out with carbolic soap.'

'Sorry.'

'I don't know where you heard a word like that. Not in this house.'

'Still, it's not fair.' Ronnie pushed past his mother at the kitchen sink and went out of the back door, his eyes filling with tears. He sat on the step facing the air raid shelter and put his head on his knees. It wasn't fair. The heat made the back garden stifling, even though it was in shade; it was a glorious Saturday – and the last before school re-opened on Monday. It was so scorching hot that they'd talked about it on the wireless. And what was he going to have to do today? Go with his mother to Auntie Edna's and sit in her stuffy front room all afternoon. He'd be given some dusty game to play while Auntie Edna and his mum talked about 'the old days'. The two sisters would laugh and clap their hands as if they'd never heard the stories before. And what would he be doing? Being bored to death by the minute.

His head sweated on his knees and he looked up, the lump of shame still in his throat and his head starting to ache. He hated rows with his mum – but going over to Auntie Edna's for tea just wasn't fair. That sort of visiting was a Sunday thing to do; and anyway, it had been more fun when his dad was there, because the three of them would walk home across the fields from Welling and call in for a lemonade and a packet of crisps at Fanny on the Hill, the pub in the valley. It would be different if they could sit out in Auntie Edna's garden, which fanned out at the side of their house, with a pond and big, slow carp to feed. Water was always fun.

He pictured Plumstead Baths, its pool slowly settling from the session before as the swimmers were let into the cubicles along the side – those wriggly lines along the tiles at the bottom gradually getting straighter. He imagined the smell of what the attendant called 'ozone'; and thought of the moment when, in the midst of all the shouting and screaming, you jumped in the deep end and it went suddenly quiet, you were all on your own, with no one else in the world. That's what he should be doing today, after a game on the common with Don Stewart's leather football, and *not* going over to stupid Auntie Edna's.

August was over, and so was summer as far as sport went. Cricket had finished and, sweltering heat or not, the football season would begin today. In about half an hour.

He'd had his dinner. And being the man of the house these days just as his dad said he had to be, he'd dried up and put everything away. And then he and his mum had had the quarrel.

'You know why I go over there! It's not for my pleasure, I can tell you! It's because of her nerves. Uncle Len's on a Saturday shift, and she's left on her own. If you had a sister, you'd want to look after her, wouldn't you?'

Ronnie wasn't so sure that he would – not when he was grown up and as old as those two. If he had a sister with such fear of tight spaces that she was forced to go upstairs on buses and trams, she ought to be in a special home.

But then he'd probably have to visit her on a Saturday afternoon…

And what a sight-and-a-half that had been last Saturday! He could still see the puffs of black smoke as a Jerry Messerschmitt had been hit by ack-ack guns and a wing fell off. The plane had spun down like a great sycamore seed – with no sign of a pilot jumping out on a parachute – until it crashed into the gardens behind Ann Street. Everything was so slow, twisting down to death – and bringing a taste of salty spit into Ronnie's mouth that he'd always remember.

This was what the war had been like so far. The odd raid, stray German planes, the air raid siren making everyone in the Anderson shelter jump, and then the all-clear going. Now and then something exciting happened, like that Messerschmitt, but otherwise, not a lot round there. All the same, his mum would take her gas mask to Auntie Edna's, and so would he – but they'd hide them in the porch before Auntie Edna opened the door. One look at a gas mask case and her nerves would come jangling out again.

The back door opened. His mother loomed over him. She'd taken off her overall and was drying her neck after her wash. 'I'm just going to put my face on, then we're going. Let's have a look at your knees.' Auntie Edna always remarked on Ronnie's nice clean knees.

'I don't want to go,' Ronnie croaked. 'It's too hot.'

'You're coming, if only as a punishment. I shan't forget what you said today. Come on!'

Ronnie slowly got up. There wasn't much sky to be seen from their back garden, but what he could see was as clear and blue as some deep lagoon asking to be dived into. He closed his eyes in the glare. It wasn't fair!

'Get a move on.' His mother was holding the back door open. 'I want to be there for three o'clock.'

Three o'clock till six, then another three-quarters of an hour on two buses to get back home again – nearly four hours of the best sunshine shining down while he was stuck indoors with Auntie Edna! And he was eleven, not a titchy infant. He was going up into Mr Rosewarn's class on Monday. 'You're a man now,' his dad had written in a letter. Well, he *was* a man – and he'd do handy jobs in the house, and he'd fight a German if he came through the door, and he'd go out to work as soon as the school let him. That was the sort of man he was. Not the sort who sat listening to Auntie Edna on account of her nerves.

A weird feeling suddenly rushed up through his body. It started somewhere down below and it rose up through him like a fountain, clearing the lump in his throat and flooding into his head, leaving it numb and cold. And it was someone else's voice that he heard as he walked past his mother into the hallway and out through the front door.

'I'm not coming. I'll see you when you get back,' he said.

And he slammed the door and walked off down Flaxton Road.

Chapter Two

Ronnie ran down the left wing, taking the ball in his stride. He looked every bit the winger, tallish for his age, slim but hard, eyes sharp as he concentrated on the ball, pushing it on a yard, and with a sure left foot he hit it over into the penalty area – where Don Stewart completely misjudged it. He tripped over the leather lump and sent his boot sailing towards the goal – which the goalie saved.

'Rotten pitch!' he shouted, kicking his other boot into the ground.

What a waste of a good cross! But it was Don's ball and Don's game – a pick-up match on the common between the gang of boys who went looking for a game on a Saturday: cricket up to last week, and now football. With all the young teachers off fighting the war, there was no one to run Saturday morning games any more. And there weren't many kids about, anyway. Ronnie and his friends were some of the left-overs who hadn't been evacuated out of London with the school. Their parents had decided to 'wait-and-see' before sending them away. When the bombing really started, they might go looking for safety in the country. But as time went on, and with the RAF in control up there, most air raid warnings were followed by empty skies. So Ronnie was still here, still going to Ancona Road Elementary School because they'd closed Timbercroft Lane and made it into a fire station.

In any case, he had his mum to look after – which, from now on, would *not* always include going with her to Auntie Edna's. He knew what his dad thought of his mum's sister. He might get a clump round the head for what he'd said today, but there was no way his dad would go on sitting in that front room in Welling when Uncle Len wasn't there.

Ronnie's dad had been called up into the Royal Artillery, and they'd had Forces Post Office letters from 'somewhere hot and wet'. The letters came with thick black ink hiding some of the things he'd written, and Ronnie understood why. The big word going round was *hush-hush*, and that's what his dad was doing, something *hush-hush* – somewhere out east, Ronnie reckoned. But this war wouldn't last long. He'd soon come marching home.

Don Stewart's mother wouldn't let Don be evacuated, either – even if Adolf Hitler came riding a tank along Plumstead Common Road. She always made a face if you didn't call him 'Donald' – and Donald Andrew Stewart was never going to be looked after by a stranger in some far-off part of the country. Mrs Stewart had heard that lots of evacuees were made to sleep *under* the beds, while the people's own children slept on top. And one little girl in the paper had accidentally been killed by being put in a bath of scalding water – no mother would ever do that. So Donald was going to stay in Plumstead.

And then there was Terry Boulter, who'd been evacuated with the school to a village in Kent when war was declared. A year ago, almost to the day, he'd gone marching bravely with their class to Plumstead station, his gas mask box round his neck, a label on his coat, and a parcel of spare pants and socks in his arms. But he didn't last long away from London. His mother went to get him at Christmas because she couldn't bear reading letters in which he called the woman in the Kent house 'Mum'.

'C'mon!' shouted Roy Bull. 'Let's have one!'

'No. Let's have our tea!' Terry shouted back. 'I'm going out tonight.'

The game had died, which was just what Ronnie didn't want. He didn't have a tea to go home to – his was over in Welling. Supper-time would be beans on toast, if he wasn't sent to bed with bread and water, but that was a long way off. So what was he going to do for the rest of the afternoon? He hadn't enough money to get into the pictures, the front wheel of his bike was punctured and he'd run out of patches, and although he could walk to Charlton Athletic football ground in time for when they opened the gates at half time, he'd always gone to Charlton with his dad, and it would be sad there without him. Besides, wartime football was all guest players and soldiers on leave – it wasn't real Charlton. Today was still bright and hot, though, and he might go blackberrying down by the allotments. Ronnie never bothered which side of a fence juicy fruit was growing.

Don's football rolled off down a slope and no one went to fetch it. Ronnie lay on the grass and looked up at the sky. He squinted his eyes and saw the great silver elephant of a barrage balloon dipping and swaying, put there to force the Jerry planes higher, to make bombing the docks or the Arsenal harder. But that Saturday, war seemed a million miles away – and what was attacking Ronnie was a large dose of boredom. And regret for what he'd done. To be honest, he hadn't enjoyed being a rebel. Every time he thought of it, his stomach took a churn.

The other boys went off to their teas and Ronnie went home. He thought about going over to Auntie Edna's late and saying sorry, but he knew that his mum would have made up some good reason why he hadn't gone, and that would mess it up for her.

Ronnie couldn't get into the house, but where he lived on the corner of Flaxton Road and Barden Street, there was a quick, easy way over the side fence into his back garden, so he could get into the air raid shelter, where he kept his model Spitfire. Anderson shelters didn't have doors – theirs had a thick blackout curtain, and inside were two bunk beds, one for his mum on top, and one for him underneath, and a kitchen chair on each side of a card table where he'd left the model he was painting. Well, he could get on with that, although he wished it was a raffia basket he was finishing, something he could give his mum to make up.

It was good having the Anderson in the garden. Covered with the earth they'd dug out to put it in, it was like having a camouflaged camp, like Robin Hood in Sherwood Forest. Ronnie kept his torch out there and his penknife and a collection of comics he hadn't read, saving them for an emergency – like an air raid, or a gas attack. But today was an emergency, wasn't it? When he'd finished painting his Spitfire out in the sun, he'd sit on top of the shelter and have a read.

'If they were going to gas us, they'd have done it by now,' Uncle Len always said. Gas was what worried people most. Auntie Edna's husband was a tall man with a pipe, excused from being called up for the forces because he worked in the Arsenal on something secret. When Uncle Len took his pipe out of his mouth to say something to you, you listened – things like, 'If Hitler drops gas on us, he knows what we'll send back – with brass knobs on.' And while Ronnie could only guess what diabolical things Uncle Len was helping to invent, he believed every word he said.

While he was saying these comforting things, Uncle Len always gave a little look at Auntie Edna.

In fact, everyone gave little looks at Auntie Edna to see that she was all right. Ronnie was even looking at her in his head as he walked home up Flaxton Road, because *she'd* caused all the trouble today; and the trouble wasn't over yet, he knew that. There was a long word for what was wrong with her, but his mum just called it nerves. Ever since they'd been girls, Edna had had her nerves. She was only a bit older than Ivy, but she didn't go out to work. Instead, she kept her house 'immaculate' (that was her word for it) – so tidy, that if you rubbed the velour on the settee the wrong way, she'd stretch across and stroke it back into place.

Ronnie's mum worked. She was up at the Optical Buildings in Garland Road – also *hush-hush* – grinding lenses for gunsights. So Ronnie was allowed into the house with his own key for half an hour after school – but not on Saturdays.

When he got there, it was still hot in the back garden, and for fear of the enamel paint drying too fast, he finished off the Spitfire inside the Anderson. But it was gloomy down there on his own; and when he looked at the sewing-box full of emergency comics tied up with one of his mum's tight knots, he decided to leave them where they were. Besides, after sweating on the common in the football match, there was only one place to be on a scorching afternoon like this – down at Plumstead Baths. He hadn't enough coppers to get into the pictures, but he had enough for a swim, and his costume and towel were still hanging on the line from the day before. There'd be plenty of time for a swim before his mum came home.

He rolled his costume and towel into a sausage and climbed back over the fence. Through the front window he could see the time on the mantelpiece clock. Twenty past four. If he was back just before six o'clock, that would be about right. There were two pools at Plumstead, the bigger, first-class one, and the second-class pool – but the first had shut down, and Uncle Len had told Ronnie why, with his pipe out of his mouth on account of what he was saying: 'Public mortuary, for all the bodies if Jerry bombs us.' But he made sure Auntie Edna didn't hear.

Ronnie hurried down Flaxton Road, a clear picture in his head of the small pool with the diving boards, where he was going to bomb into the deep end. He could almost taste the water – a taste that suddenly changed to salt as he heard them coming over: aircraft. Definitely aircraft. And not RAF, either.

These planes had a chugging drone that told him there were Jerries up there. And just as he heard them, the air raid siren on the school roof made him jump him with its start-up whine, like some creature clearing its throat. Together the two sounds were terrifying: the wail of the alert which grabbed at his guts, and the growl of the German Air Force coming at him. This was no hit-and-run nuisance raid. This was war for real: the thundering of the engines told him that.

Ronnie ran. An air raid warden came pelting out of Kirkham Street shouting, 'Take cover! Take cover!' Ronnie looked around. *Take cover where?* In someone's doorway, or back home in the Anderson?

The Warden was waving and pointing. 'Get to the shelter on the common!'

Ronnie ducked his head and sprinted for it, a hundred yards away at the bottom of Flaxton Road. He looked up as he ran. In the sky above him the Jerries were spread across like a heavy black curtain, hundreds of them clouding the sun. And his heart jumped again as he saw a stick of bombs coming screeching down on Plumstead. He spurted across the road to where people were rushing into the public shelter – when suddenly the ground shook.

As a huge bomb exploded somewhere near, the blast of it rocking him with a force that seemed to be sucking out his breath and his eyeballs. Coughing and spitting, he got into the shelter just before the next bomb landed. It shook the walls and brought concrete dust showering down over everyone.

'Good gawd!' an old man said, as his wife knocked the dust out of his hair. 'We're catching a packet! Like the Somme.'

A little girl was screaming, her mother leaning over her for protection.

A string of explosions ran on down towards the river, *thud, thud, thud, thud.*

'They're after the Arsenal.'

'They're after more'n that. Listen to how many there are up there.'

Everyone in the shelter listened to the noise of those heavy, throbbing engines, hundreds of them, wave after wave of bomb-laden aircraft, the whistle and thud of death coming down, the pom-pom of defensive guns, and the howl of swooping planes as Spitfires and Heinkels fought like dogs.

No one in the shelter had put their gas masks on. Ronnie hadn't got his, anyway. With another enormous thud, nearer still, the ground shook and cement fell out of the shelter's brickwork.

'It's the end of the world!' a young woman wailed.

'It's the start of the real stuff,' said the old soldier. 'They mean business today.'

Ronnie looked at the concrete slab above his head, set across the top of the thick brick walls. The shelter felt safe, although nothing would save them from a direct hit – they'd just be blown to smithereens. But having got in, Ronnie suddenly wanted to be out.

'My mum!' he shouted. 'She's out in this. She's gone to Welling on the bus...' He got up and headed for the entrance.

'Stay where you are, son!' The old soldier was on his feet. 'What good are you gonna do her if she's out in it?'

'I'll be with her!' Ronnie dodged the old man's hands. If he was going to get killed, he wasn't going to die without making up his quarrel with his mother.

'Don't be a young fool!' The old man got hold of him, and the wife was coming to help – but Ronnie wrenched himself free and ran from the shelter. He'd got two good legs, hadn't he? And he'd promised his dad he would look after his mum. The buses would have stopped – but he could easily run to Welling…

He'd just have to dodge the bombs.

Chapter Three

But it wasn't just the bombs. What Ronnie hadn't bargained for were the flying slates, the daggers of glass, and the shrapnel pinging about like bullets. It was all dust and smoke. Looking up, he could see the crosses on the Jerry wings, and the bomb racks opening. So he pelted back the way he'd come, on towards Welling.

He took a left turn – and came to a halt. This wasn't Rush Street any more! Where the first bomb had fallen, houses were spewed across the road and firemen were hosing into the rafters of the buildings. Policemen were leading people away, bloodied and blackened, one of them a baby girl carried by her mother. The sight twisted Ronnie's stomach and made his heart thump – while his lungs choked up with the smoke and dust.

But what about his mum? Could this be happening to her? He ran out of the streets and headed across the fields. He jumped the banks of the dried-up Quaggy river and ran on towards the wider roads of Welling. Above him the Spitfires, Hurricanes and Messerschmitts were fighting their own battles – and the sudden sight of a parachute coming down caught Ronnie's eye. Invasion? Could this be the invasion? Were the Germans softening them up with bombs, then sending down their paratroops?

He ran on. He had to get to Auntie Edna's to be with his mum. But as he ran he kept looking up – and saw that it wasn't a man's shape on the parachute, but a round thing. It had to be a bomb. People in steel helmets shouted at him – a policeman and another warden.

'Take cover!'

'Get into a shelter, you stupid kid!'

But no one was going to put Ronnie off. The air was thick with black and yellow smoke, the ground kept shaking with high explosives – and as he ran into Wickham Street, a thunderous burst threw him half across the road. The parachute bomb had landed. Again, the air was sucked out of him and he pressed his eyeballs hard in the blast, stumbling blindly into Auntie Edna's road, where his mother would be.

And – help! – dear God! A bomb had already fallen. The road was cordoned off, and halfway down on the right he could see people and vehicles and stripped trees, with sheets and curtaining caught like ghosts in the branches. He stood, stared, and spat acid. Halfway down on the right was where Auntie Edna lived.

'Mum!' He charged forward, dodging his way through rubble, glass and felled branches, racing to where the bomb had fallen. A policeman grabbed at him, a soldier shouted, an ambulance woman looked up from a casualty on the pavement – but no one was going to stop Ronnie Warren. 'Mum! Mum!' He had never seen things so clearly in his life, everything was precision-sharp. He ran on to where Auntie Edna's house had been standing – and still was! Just. It was there, its side wall tilting over at a mad angle. But it wasn't the house he was staring at: it was the garden beside it, where Uncle Len had dug in their air raid shelter. There was nothing now but a huge crater as wide as Plumstead bath – and deep, with black smoke curling out of it, like looking down into hell.

'Oi!' The policeman had caught up with Ronnie, had his shoulder in a no-nonsense grip. 'What's your game?'

'My mum. It's my mum. She was in my auntie's shelter.'

'Where's that?'

'Down there. Down that hole.'

'Ah. Well, you come over here.' He pulled Ronnie firmly across to the other side of the road where the houses were still standing. 'Come on, son.' The policeman looked for the Warden. 'ARP? – this lad'll have names.'

The Air Raid Warden – an older man with an armband – came over, fishing out a pad and a pencil. 'What number?' he asked Ronnie.

'Two. My mum and my Auntie Edna.'

'No, what number on the door?'

'That one there.' Auntie Edna's looked like a haunted house on a fairground, tottery and tumbly, but its number was still screwed to the brickwork at the front. 'Fifteen. "Lenedna". 'My mum was here, and my auntie...'

'What were their names, son?'

'Ivy Warren – my mum, and Edna... Pearce.' *The man had said 'were'.* And giving his mother's name like that suddenly smacked the truth on to Ronnie's face like a teacher's slap. His mum and her sister were *weres*.

'Two r's in Warren?'

Ronnie nodded, and crouched down on the pavement.

'And they'd have been in the air raid shelter, wouldn't they?' the policeman asked.

Along the middle of the road between Ronnie and number fifteen they were running a rope with a sign hanging on it: DANGEROUS STRUCTURE – KEEP OUT. Along to his left, men and women were pulling bricks from a mound of rubble that had once been the next house down the road. A whistle blew sounding silence – and everyone stopped to listen, although all that could be heard was the drone of bombers, the chase of fighters, and the sound of bombs falling somewhere over the river. The whistle blew again – and people scrabbled at the rubble once more.

'I said, they'd have been in the shelter, wouldn't they? Not shopping, not indoors…?'

'Shelter…' Ronnie croaked, as a great heave of breath caught him. His mum was dead. He didn't have a mother any more.

Except... Not shelter: Auntie Edna hated it. Forget the *weres* of the Warden. What had the policeman said? Shopping? Indoors? Ronnie knew that his mum and Auntie Edna hadn't gone shopping. So could they be in the house?

He looked across the road. Instead of going down the dark shelter, had they stayed indoors and hidden under the table in Auntie Edna's dining-room? Could they still be in there...?

Ronnie jumped up. 'They could be indoors!' he told the policeman.

'You've changed your tune. Why not in the shelter?'

'Because my auntie doesn't like dark places. Nerves, my mum says. Come on!' Ronnie tried to run across the road, but the policeman pulled him back.

'You're not going into that premises, son. See the sign? That house is coming down any second. Collapsing. One blast within a mile and the whole caboosh'll shake down into dust...'

'But if they're in there...'

'That don't alter a thing. We're not going into Number Fifteen until heavy rescue gets here, and you're not neither.'

Ronnie slumped; but not inside. Inside,

Ronnie Warren was in charge, and knew what he was doing; it was what he did when he played kiss chase and prisoners were taken. He would shrink, go small and seem to give in until the grip weakened on him – then suddenly wriggle out and get away.

'OK,' he said – and turned away.

'Makes sense, son,' the policeman said. 'Heavy rescue could be here any minute…'

But Ronnie had gone. With a sudden dip, he twisted back and was already running for the security rope, hurdling it, heading for the house.

No one was going to stop him from getting to his mother.

Chapter Four

The front door was half open. As Ronnie ran for it, the policeman grabbed at his shoulder and the Warden tried to cut him off – but tripped over the rope and brought the officer down. Heading for the porch, Ronnie could see the crazy angle of the front wall, the window bowing out, and the upstairs hanging a yard and a half over him before he even got there.

He took a deep breath and pushed inside, where the dust hung as thick as smoke, clogging his lungs. He couldn't see; but he somehow managed to shout, 'Mum! Mum! Are you in there?' He listened, but heard nothing.

Outside, a whistle was blowing, and a voice was shouting, 'Come out, you little fool!

Get out while you can!'

Ronnie groped his way along the hallway towards the second door. He knew the house. The first door would be the front room. But nothing inside looked like Auntie Edna's right now: the hallstand was broken in two, the ceiling was down, and there was wall plaster all over the floor. He knew where the dining-room was, with the big oak table in the middle. That's where they'd be. He pushed the second door, but the uprights weren't upright any more – and who knew what would happen to the upstairs if he pushed it too hard? The whole lot might come crashing down on him.

'Mum! Mum! Auntie Edna!' He didn't want to shout too loudly in case his voice set off vibrations. Somehow he squeezed through the door without moving it too much.

'Mum! Mum!'

The back wall and window of the dining-room no longer existed. Over there, the ceiling dipped to within a foot of the floor. The room lay in dark shadows. Bending to get further in, Ronnie could see a dressing-table on the grass outside, its mirrors shattered, drawers scattered, and strips of bedding all over the ground. And he could see feet outside, heavy boots – the policeman and the others had come round to the back.

'Oi! Son! Get the hell out! Quick!'

The whole place was upside-down; but the dining table stood solid, Auntie Edna's best table-cloth hung tattered under plaster and glass, all the tassles torn and stringy. Half-afraid to look, Ronnie bent down to squint beneath it.

What was that? What were they?

They were legs. Women's legs at weird angles, lying still, and on the feet nearest him were his mother's shoes. Next to them, in torn, bloody stockings, were the curled-up legs of Auntie Edna. They were here!

'Mum! Mum!'

Ronnie got down on his hands and knees and crawled across brick and plaster to get round to the other side of the table.

His mum was lying still, making no sound. He hardly dared to look. What was he going to find when he saw her face?

Suddenly the house shifted with a great creak.

'She's going!' shouted someone outside. 'Stand back! The blighter's coming down!'

'Are you in there, son?' It was the policeman,

peering under the fallen upstairs floor.

Ronnie scrambled round to his mother, her arms as awkward as her legs, her dead-looking face covered in brick-dust and blood. Mum! Dear Mum! And the last thing he'd ever said to her had had no love in it. Whatever state she was in, injured or dead, she would always be his mum. He spat on his fingers and wiped the dust off her face, put his cheek to hers, the way he'd seen people do in films.

And she was warm! He looked into her eyes. There was no opening them with all the débris on her eyelids – but did one of them twitch? Across the room lay a floor joist from upstairs, which must have hit her.

'Mum! Mum!'

The house creaked and it shifted again, bits of bedroom crashing down outside, and people were shouting.

'Stand clear there!'

'Stand away! She's coming down.'

Ronnie had to get his mother out. He knew you shouldn't move someone who could be bleeding inside, but what else could he do? No one was coming in to get them. And suddenly it wasn't dark any more. He could see the sky. At ground level there was one small gap where the upstairs hadn't come down. Desperately Ronnie lifted his mother's body and pushed his cut, grazed hands under her armpits. He got himself into a crouching position, and pulled at her. And as he pulled, she groaned.

Thank you, God!

With every muscle straining, he pulled her inch by inch across the rubble of the floor towards the gap leading to the outside – where a head was bent, a face staring through.

'Leave her, son! You'll never do it. Leave her! Save yourself.' It was the policeman – whose shout unsettled the fragile structure even more. Slates slid and crashed, and the floorboards beneath Ronnie dipped with the skew of the house.

'It's going! It's gonna go!'

With a sudden burst of brick and débris, the chimney-stack crashed into the room. But right now Ronnie had the strength of his father as he took a fresh grip on his mother, and pulled and pulled. If the lot came down now, he'd be under it with her; but there was no chance on earth he'd leave her. No chance in heaven or hell.

He pulled – and she was coming. A deep breath, and he pulled again, and dragged her towards the small opening – where the brave policeman's face remained, calling a different message now.

'Not far. Not far, son – here, give us that arm.'

He was nearly there – when the building took another shudder. This would be the last pull, he knew it.

'Her arm! Give us her arm!'

The policeman's hand was reaching in. Ronnie lifted his mother's right arm round above her head so the policeman could grab it – and with a mighty tug, bumped and whimpering now, his mother was pulled through the gap, her shoes ripped off and her legs bleeding with new cuts.

Now it was his turn.

But what was that shrieking?

'Take cover!'

'Get your heads down!'

'Lie flat!'

It was the terrifying whistle of a bomb screeching out of the sky. There'd be a great shake of the earth at any second, and that would be the end. Already the gap to the outside looked impossibly small.

But the policeman was back. He was reaching in for Ronnie. And as their hands met, a huge explosion and an almighty crunch heaved the ground beneath them, followed by a blast, and a terrifying suck. The house caved in on itself as the policeman pulled, and Ronnie flew through the gap to land on top of his mother on the grass, with the man thrown across the two of them.

There was no hearing, no seeing, and none of them moved. Who was alive? Who was dead? Gradually, as the shock waves passed, and the dust swirled, Ronnie realised that he was breathing and alive. He opened his eyes, and there was rubble across his legs, but they moved when he tried them, and beneath him his mother started to cough.

The policeman slowly got off them. 'You little fool!' he said to Ronnie. 'You know what you've done? You've made me dent my whistle.'

And he had. The policeman's whistle was a piece of flat tin. The house was a mound of débris; and civil defence would have to wait for heavy rescue to come to dig for Auntie Edna.

'But you're a brave little tyke, I'll say that...'

✗✗✗

'He'll get a medal for what he did.'

Ivy Warren was lying in bed in the Memorial

hospital, her voice a thin croak. 'They'll give that policeman a George Medal for what he's done, or I'm a Dutchman.'

Ronnie nodded. He patted her hand, the one bit of her he was allowed to touch. Her head seemed to be held together by a tight crêpe bandage; her right arm was in a sling; and her legs must be bad, because the bedclothes were kept off them by a frame.

Ronnie was choked. 'I'm sorry about Auntie Edna,' he said.

'She was my sister.' His mother spoke simply, like a child.

'Yeah.' He looked into her eyes. 'And I'm sorry about... you know ...'

She stared back before closing her eyes, then slowly opened them again. 'You started the day like a silly little boy,' she said, 'but you finished it like a man, Ronnie Warren.'

Which made Ronnie want to cry. He didn't know what to say.

'That's what war does,' his mother said. 'That ... is war.' And as she said it, the air raid alert went again. She looked up at the ceiling. 'God help us. The blighters are coming back.'

That was all they had time to say to each other before Ronnie and the other visitors started helping the nurses push the beds, to evacuate the casualty department down to the hospital basement.

The Blitz had begun.

Top Bunk Boy

Chapter One

'What's your name?'

'Ronnie, sir.'

'Your full name!' The teacher, who had just come in and hung his cane on the back of the classroom door, didn't even look at the piece of paper Ronnie gave him. 'Ronnie wha', lad?'

'Warren.'

'Sir.'

'Warren, sir.'

'Bunny, bunny, bunny, bunny…' came a murmuring from the back of the room. Ronnie clenched his jaw and stayed looking at the teacher.

'Sit o'er there, then, War-ren.' Mr Kirkham pointed to a seat at the side of the class, next to a big kid with a smirk.

Warren! Ronnie had never been 'Warren' in London: he'd been 'Ronnie' – or 'Ronald' if his teacher wasn't pleased with him. But up here in the north, things were very different from back home. The old classroom had steps of desks up to the back wall, and the fourteen-year-olds waiting to leave school – like this one next to him – were in the same class as the ones who'd be taking the Scholarship. He sat where he was told, on the outside of a double desk on the third tier, where his smirking partner was lolling against the wall with a shiny face and spiteful eyes – and pinched Ronnie's backside as he sat down. Sharp nails.

'Didn't hurt!' he lied to the boy.

'Talk-ing!' Mr Kirkham shouted. He was heading their way, and for a moment Ronnie thought he was going to be cuffed round the head. Instead, two used exercise books were thumped on to the desk top, and a pencil and a pen clattered into their groove. 'Cross out t'other name, an' start a fresh page wi' your'n at top. A-rithmetic an' English.'

Ronnie knew paper was scarce. The stuff they made it from had to be brought into the docks from abroad, and ships were being sunk all the time. So a lot of rubbing-out went on. The boy whose name was on the book must have left school.

'D'you know your tables?'

'Yes, sir.'

The man stood leaning his weight on the desk with his hand spread across the back of the arithmetic exercise book, where the tables were printed.

'Eight sevens?'

'Fifty-six.' Ronnie's dad had sat with him night after night when Ronnie was due to take tests.

'Stand up!'

Ronnie stood.

'Mek a fist.'

Ronnie made a fist, as the teacher picked up a ruler from a girl's desk across the aisle. He gripped Ronnie's wrist and hit his knuckles with the ruler's edge, three times. 'Fifty... six... sir!' He threw Ronnie's arm back at him like a discarded stick. 'Nine eights?'

'Seventy-two.' Ronnie kept his voice normal, waited until the man snatched in his breath and grabbed the ruler again, before he stuck 'sir' on the end.

'Tha's better.' But the teacher's eyes said he wasn't so sure. He returned to his desk at the front and opened the register. He was older than Ronnie's dad but not as old as a granddad, with oiled grey hair parted down the middle of his head. His face was as craggy as a rock cake.

Ronnie sat up like the rest of the class, straight backed, arms folded across his chest. The last thing he was going to do was nurse his bruised knuckles, but he could feel them glowing red.

'Register.' Mr Kirkham ran his currant eyes around the room as he unscrewed the cap of his pen. But when he put on his glasses and looked down at the register, the girl across the aisle leant across for her ruler, which had been left on Ronnie's desk.

'Ta,' she said in a voice as soft as breath. Ronnie swivelled his eyes towards her. She didn't grab the ruler but took it quietly, looking at it with a frown as if she was disappointed with what it had just done. She was nice. Her hair was in two plaits that reached below her shoulders, the nearer one in front, the other behind her pinafore top. She was facing the front again, but Ronnie could see that her eyes were blue, with long lashes, emphasised by the way she slowly blinked.

Mr Kirkham kept them waiting, adding Ronnie's name to the bottom of the boys' section of the register and blotting it, before calling each surname, to which the boys replied, 'Present, sir.' Until he came to 'Warren'. Which was when Ronnie asked for what he got; because instead of replying 'Present, sir,' like the rest, he lifted his head with a stupid surge of London pride and called out the way he would at Ancona Road School. 'Here!' – adding 'sir,' as the man got to his feet and came at him like a snorting bull.

He grabbed Ronnie by his shirt collar, tearing it. 'Wha' is it wi' you?' he demanded. 'Showing off your cocky southern ways? Ye've go' a lesson or two to learn, laddie!' He thumped him in the back. 'Wha? Wha' have you got to learn?' he bent to shout into his face.

'A lesson, sir.'

'Right!' The man straightened.

'Or two.'

Mr Kirkham had started to move back to the front. Now he was caught in mid-step. For a second he teetered, before straightening his neck and walking back to his desk. Ronnie looked round at the girl across the aisle, who smiled briefly – giving Ronnie his first little lift since last Saturday, when his mother had brought him up north.

Chapter Two

'You're goin' te behave yourself while you're wi' me. I've got rules. Rules for me own, lad, an' they'll do for you. For a start, I'll have no bad language – I know you London lot.'

The woman tucked in her chin and stared across the table at Ronnie. Her name was Mrs Barton – Mrs Barton Number Two. Mrs Barton Number One was the woman who'd opened the door to Ronnie and his mother, who'd smiled at both of them and carried Ronnie's suitcase upstairs. She had shown him where he'd be sleeping – on the bottom bunk in a small bedroom over the front door – and she'd counted out Ronnie's rent for the first month, and put on her glasses to check through his ration book.

'Best to be sure before the off,' she'd told Ronnie's mother. 'I'll register him with my grocer first thing come Monday.' The ration book was slipped into a kitchen drawer. 'Meanwhile, he c'n eat out of ours. He's no massive eater, I'm thinkin'.' She had smiled at Ronnie's mother, but lost the smile by the time she'd fixed her eyes on Ronnie's skinny body – changing instantly from being Mrs Barton-Number-One-the-kindly-landlady to Mrs-Barton-Number-Two-the-mill-worker who could mind any man's machine.

The three of them were sitting around the kitchen table making contact with talk of the heavy London Blitz and the local incendiary bomb that had fallen up the road at Ashton Under Ribble. Ronnie's mouth opened to say something, but his mother's eyes pierced him, and he shut it again fast. He might have saved his mother's life, but she was still the one who knew best.

'So who will Ronnie be sharing the bunk bed with?' his mother wanted to know.

'It's Eric's room, my eldest, fifteen an' working on' railway. We've got the double bunk in especially. He's a good 'un, is Eric. You lads'll get on like a house a'fire. He doesn't smoke, an' he keeps himself immaculate clean' – with a quick look at Ronnie's finger-nails.

Mrs Warren had cut them herself that morning. 'Good,' she said, 'Ronnie's a nice clean boy, too.' She looked at her watch, making an anxious face, a look Ronnie knew well. She'd got to leave soon, to get the bus to Preston station for the London train, and they'd both have liked a bit of time on their own. Saying goodbye should be private. On the way north she'd told Ronnie how grown-up he had to be, and how she'd be all right in London because Uncle Len would 'keep an eye'. But before she left him, he knew there was a hug and a kiss and a cry to come. Meanwhile, Mrs Barton went on and on, using up the time like spilling precious milk – all about how Sergeant Barton was in charge of a searchlight somewhere secret on the south coast. 'An' I'll lay there's southern folk on searchlights up here!' And she spoke about her willingness to help out in these bad times by taking in a kiddie who'd been bombed out of house and home. Ronnie's mother's sad look across at her son said she was claiming poor Auntie Edna's house as their own disaster.

In the end, Ronnie's mother had to ask to take

him upstairs to the bedroom to check that he'd got everything.

But Mrs Barton saw through that. 'Don't go mekin' him cry, love. We don't want tears, now, there's no need. He's goin' to be champion wi' me.'

The two Londoners bravely came up to scratch. There was just time for a quick hug, a persuasive, 'She seems a very pleasant woman,' – and after one last kiss, Ronnie's mother went off along the terrace towards the bus stop with only the slightest of limps, her handkerchief to her mouth as if she had toothache in a cold wind.

As the door was quietly shut on her, Mrs Barton Number One turned into Mrs Barton Number Two. 'Ye c'n wash these cups an' saucers, lad,' she said. 'An' watch your backside if ye break owt.'

✗✗✗

It was peculiar, being in someone else's house. At home in London Ronnie had the run of the place. If he fancied a crust of bread, he'd sneak into the kitchen. If he wanted to read a comic up at the table, he'd spread his elbows. Or if he thought he'd lay out his train set in the front room, he'd get down to where he could smell the carpet and roughen his knees. It was his house, where he lived. But here at Mrs Barton's, he was a visitor who couldn't just wander about as if he owned the place. The front room looked out of bounds. Even his mother hadn't been taken in there – they'd sat in the kitchen. The dining-room had a table, chairs and a dresser, but nothing 'knocking about' in the same way there was at home – no newspapers under the cushions or bits of paper tucked behind the clock. And nowhere was there anything for Ronnie to do. His model Spitfire was still in London waiting for the RAF markings to be transferred on to the wings. All he'd brought in his pocket was his favourite Dinky toy car – a maroon Humber – and upstairs in his suitcase there was a Just William book he'd read twice. But right now he didn't want to read, and his car might scratch the dining-room table, with no oilcloth on it. So he carefully washed and dried the cups and saucers and, while Mrs Barton went though his ration book again like a suspicious grocer, he took himself upstairs to the bedroom he was going to share with Eric.

As he climbed the stairs, he couldn't help thinking that going to Auntie Edna's would have been a rare treat compared with this.

It seemed as if Eric lived a lodger's life, too. Nothing much in the room said *Eric*. If he had any books, they were in the dressing-table or the wardrobe – and with its key in the lock, Ronnie dared not open it. Both the bunk beds were made up, but neither of them had an eiderdown – just grey blankets, like a barracks. There was a mirror to the dressing-table and an ancient painting on the wall of an old man in breeches looking out of a window at a tree; and on the iron mantelpiece there was a silver ashtray. The floor was linoleum, with a strip of mat where their feet would touch getting out of the bunk bed. The room looked just as *nothing* as downstairs.

He opened his suitcase with two exploding cracks that he thought might bring Mrs Barton up from the kitchen. But they didn't, and he was all right – just about all right – until he saw it, lying across the top of his packed clothes – a piece of paper that hadn't been there before. His mother must have put it there last thing before she went.

Ronnie – be a good boy for Mrs Barton. Make Dad and me proud of you. This rotten old war will soon be over and we'll all be together again like before.

*Remember, you're my hero son. Chin up,
Ron. Happy days will come again.*

Your loving Mum xxx

And that did it. Ronnie sat on the bed and cried,
and in the depths of his misery he cursed Hitler and
all the Germans for what they were doing to him
and his family.

He didn't hear the bedroom door open.

'Hey-up! We got a s-s-s-southern s-s-s-softie
'ere, 'ave we?'

Ronnie rubbed his eyes, and squinted at the
other boy. This had to be Eric. He was in a tight suit,
collar and tie, and black boots. He was spotty, with
Brylcreemed hair and a side parting, not very tall,
standing with his arms folded like a foreman,
his mouth tight and pouty, just right for having
a cigarette stuck in it.

Ronnie stood up. 'No, I'm all right. Got something
in my eye.' He was taller than this working man
Eric Barton.

Eric stared back at him, and in silence took off
his collar and tie in one movement, and put the

studs in the silver ashtray on the mantelpiece, dropped them in, *clink, clink*. 'T-t-t-top bunk's … mine.' He took off his jacket and hung it in the wardrobe, pulled out a cardigan to replace it. 'An' d-d-don' leave that case sticking out where I c'n t-t-trip on it. I'll be up an' out afore ye go t' school.'

Ronnie pushed the case under the bed with his foot. 'You've done your buttons up wrong,' he said.

'Wha'?'

'Your cardigan. You're up on one side.'

'Just the way I l-like it.' Eric went out, closing the door quietly behind him – although when Ronnie followed him downstairs for tea, he saw that he'd done it up right.

Chapter Three

The game was buzz-ball. In London they called it 'king-ey', but it was the same game, and Ronnie had always been good at it. One person was king-ey and started with the ball, aiming it at someone, who joined in on the attack if he was hit, bouncing and passing the ball for a shot at someone else. The winner was the last one to be hit. Played by the boys, it took over the playground until the cricket season, leaving the girls to skip in the alcoves, or play ball against the walls. And this was one of Ronnie's 'king-ey' tricks – to stand casually among the girls until there were so few others to aim at that he had to show himself as a target.

But that first playtime at Easington Street School,

he didn't try any tricks. Like the others, he ran in the opposite direction to the ball, showing himself to make it obvious he was playing by wrapping his handkerchief round his right hand, ready to punch the ball away. But the game went in other directions for the first five minutes, and no one took a shot at him. So, as the numbers of attackers went up and there were only a couple of other kids left to hit, he decided he'd better take a chance in the open. He ran across the space between two classrooms, ready to punch or jump or dodge as the boy with the ball looked around for a target.

Behind Ronnie, the big kid he sat next to held up his hands for a pass, and caught the ball. Now Ronnie took off fast, waiting for a whack in the back – only a fool would miss from there. But the kid shot at someone else, scored a hit – and everyone's arms went up to say the game was over. And Ronnie was still free.

'You never got me!' he shouted.

'Weren't in't game,' the big kid said – and the huddle of boys scattered while the next 'he' counted to ten. Ronnie stood there, hot from running, and cold from this exclusion.

'Ye c'n turn our rope,' a girl said to him, while

her friends stood and laughed.

'No, thanks.' Ronnie leant against the wall. It was a mild November day with low clouds. Rain was never far off up here. 'Auntie Barton' to live with. A cold kid in his bedroom. Knuckles rapped and a thump in the back on his first morning. A crowd of boys who hated him for not being from round here. How rotten could things get?

'You from London?' The voice was soft. It was the girl across the aisle whose ruler had been used to teach him a lesson.

'That's right.'

'Is it terrible down there?'

'My auntie got killed.' Ronnie wasn't going to show off about what he'd done.

'Bomb?'

'Yeah. but it's just, my mum does war work. Different shifts. Can't look after me...' Ronnie wouldn't want anyone to think he'd run away from anything. Far from it.

'What war work?'

'She–' Ronnie stopped. *The walls have ears,* said the posters.

'I'm not a German spy...' The girl smiled, and put a hand on his arm. 'I'm Wendy...'

'Penworth,' Ronnie said. 'I heard the register.'

'Tha's right, Wendy Penworth. An' he died…'

'Who did?'

'Lennie Earnshaw. You got his old exercise books. Scarlet fever.'

'An' this is Bunny Warren, who won't last long, neither.' A boy was suddenly leaning on the wall with an arm between Ronnie and the girl. Not Ronnie's older deskmate, but a wiry, hard-faced boy who sat at the back of the room. He poked Ronnie, hard. 'Wha' you doin' wi' him?' he demanded of Wendy.

'Talking.' She turned on the boy. 'It's a free country.'

'Well, don't. 'Less I say so.' The boy looked round to see where the buzz-ball was, and suddenly took off when it came stinging his way. It hit the wall beside Ronnie's head, and bounced off, hard.

'What's up with him?' Ronnie asked.

'Reckons he's my boyfriend.'

'Oh. Well, you tell him, if he calls me "Bunny" again, I'll flatten him.'

Wendy's eyes widened. 'No one fights Jack Harding.'

'Don't they? Perhaps not up to now…'

The whistle blew for the end of playtime, and

the classes lined up to march back into the building, a column of boys and a column of girls – with someone behind Ronnie hacking at his heels the whole way into the school. He fought to ignore it. He knew who it was. Anyway, after he'd sorted him out, this Harding kid wouldn't be doing any more niggling, that was for certain.

xxx

Eric was a funny bloke. He was all over the place. One minute he was talking football, telling Ronnie what rubbish Charlton Athletic were compared with Preston North End, 'first winners of the league an' cup double', then he would suddenly ask, 'What c-c-class y' in? At Easington?'

'Kirkham's.'

Eric's eyes went strange, squinting at Ronnie as if he were telling the biggest lie ever. 'He still there?'

'He was today.'

Eric looked hard at what he was doing, helping to clear the tea table, gathering up the cutlery, but he was quieter than he had been a few seconds before. Then: 'They g-go on that he's got a b-bit o' shrapnel in his head. F-first War.'

'Oh, yeah? Knew something was up with him.'

'Ye're dead right there.' Eric went through to the kitchen, and as Ronnie collected plates he heard him tell Auntie Barton, 'London k-kid's in K-kirkham's.'

'Oh, yes?' And there was a long silence, making Ronnie feel the need to cough as he carried things through.

Sometimes Eric was loud, at others quiet, sometimes pally, mostly not. In their bedroom, if Ronnie left a plimsoll in the middle of the floor, at one time Eric would dribble it as if it were a football and shoot it at the door, but at another, he'd pick it up and swipe it at Ronnie's head: 'Scruff-'ouse!' And if Ronnie wriggled in his bunk, it might be, 'Wey, over t-t-t'points we go,' and he'd start the bunk swaying from the top as if they were on a train. Another time, he'd put an angry face down into Ronnie's space and tell him to 'L-l-lie still, ye scratchin' fleabag.' And sometimes in the night Ronnie would hear him talking in his sleep, a sort of whining, as if he were saying sorry for something, and he never stuttered. He would end with a snort, and a croaky voice would come down, 'Ye are a-s-s-sleep, aren't ye?' And Ronnie would have to make deep breathing sounds.

He'd stare up at the underside of Eric's bunk

and wish he was on his own in London with his mother up above. Which was where she would be right now, with bombs falling all around, and him away from it all – thoughts that made him squirm in his safety – until, 'L-l-lie still, ye s-s-scratch-arse!' would come down from the top bunk.

It was not going to be easy.

Chapter Four

Ronnie could fit in at most places. When his school in Timbercroft Lane had changed on account of a fire station taking over, he'd soon settled in at Ancona Road – but then, he did have some mates who changed schools, too. It had taken those weeks in September and October for his mother to get over her bombing injuries, but as soon as she had come home, and Uncle Len could stop looking after him at Flaxton Road, this billet had been found for him in the north of England. Mrs Gritton, who worked at the Optical Buildings, knew someone who knew someone who knew Mrs Barton, who was prepared to take an evacuee from a decent home.

'You'll have to pay, and go private,' Uncle Len had told his mother. 'If the boy had gone with the school last year, it'd be different. Now it's down to you.' He tapped his pipe on his teeth, looking at Ronnie as if he was Liability Number One.

And Mum'd be dead, Ronnie had thought. But he'd said nothing – because of Auntie Edna.

Right now, he wished he was back home in the London Blitz. You could take shelter from bombs – unless you were unlucky enough to take a hit. But you couldn't protect yourself from not being liked – or hated, even. There was no warning siren to signal the on and off of that sort of loneliness. Nothing could take away the churn of knowing he was going to suffer just for being a boy from London, until he sorted things out. As he walked to the school on his second day, he passed a lorry waiting at traffic lights on the Blackpool road. It had 'London Brick Company' painted on its side; and just for a moment he was tempted to climb over the tailboard and settle in with the bricks. But he wasn't sure which way the lorry was going. Blackpool was further north, wasn't it? And what a weak thought that was for a hero. He tried to picture his mother's disappointed face when he knocked on the door of Flaxton Road, and Uncle Len's expression, pushing aside his dinner plate as Ronnie came into the living-room. No, Ronnie's job was to stay clear to let his mum do her work in the Optical Building; that was the way they'd beat Hitler.

So he had to be here, he had to stick it – for the Warrens, and for England.

It wasn't easy, in the playground, after the brick lorry had gone. A big game of buzz-ball was going on. Boys went to school early to get a game in before lessons. Like everyone else, he kept one eye out for flying balls: even a tennis 'core' could sting if it caught you when you weren't looking. But all the time he was on the lookout for Wendy Penworth. She always gave him a kind word. As usual, Wendy was with her friends in one of the alcoves, uncoiling a rope for skipping.

Whack! Someone's flat hand came stinging round his ear. "Hey-up, Bunny!" It was Derek Smeaton, the big kid who shared his desk.

'My name's—' But Smeaton had run past him into the playground to play buzz-ball, and Ronnie was left standing there. He watched as Smeaton said something to Jack Harding, saw them both looking over at him and laughing, Harding doing rabbits' ears – which called for a 'v' sign back; but before Ronnie could give them one, they ran off in different directions when the buzz-ball went close.

Right! Ronnie thought. He'd had enough of this. *It's today, then.*

So was it to be back out of the school gate and look for another London lorry? Or should he go into school and bide his time until morning break?

Well, Ronnie Warren wasn't a runner, was he? It wasn't even a fair question. With a last look over his shoulder, he walked into the school.

✕✕✕

Mrs Cassell came into their class for singing, while Mr Kirkham took her class for ruler work. But this wasn't real singing. Singing at Timbercroft Lane had always been songs: 'Pedro the Fisherman' (always whistling), and 'The Lincolnshire Poacher' (out on shiny nights in the season of the year), with Mrs Nunn conducting and the class standing and swaying and clearing their throats between playtime and going home time. But up here, for a start, music was in the morning, like Arithmetic; and there was *tonic sol-fa* instead of songs – a blackboard with *doh*, *ray, me* thrown over it on an oil-cloth chart, with Mrs Cassell pointing at the words in no particular order – and the class had to hit the right note first time. Up and down, down and up, jumping from *doh* to *soh* and *te* to *ray*, Mrs Cassell's eyes staring round the classroom as if they were what she used for listening. Then a whack on the desk for everyone to stop, when she thought she heard a wrong note, and some poor boy or girl had to do it again solo. And this time, of course, it had to be new boy Ronnie Warren – who didn't know a *doh* from a doughnut. He was commanded to stand and sing *ray* to *lah*, down there to up there, notes which he couldn't hit. He sounded like a cat in a rat-trap.

'Appalling! Dis-graceful!'

Ronnie's inside flashed with anger at Mrs Cassell's sneers – and at Jack Harding's cocky smile – but he let nothing show on his face; because he was going to sort things out at playtime. And Wendy Penworth's sympathetic little 'Ahh...' across the aisle suddenly told him how he was going to start doing it.

✗✗✗

Buzz-ball was taking up most of the playground, but Wendy and her friends were skipping in the first alcove. As usual, the boys had their eyes on the ball as they ran their loops and spurts, but Ronnie knew Jack Harding also had his eye on him.

Ronnie went over to Wendy, who was waiting in line to run into the rope.

'Got a mo?' he asked.

'What for?'

'I want a word.'

'A'right.' Wendy came out of the line and walked over to Ronnie, who backed out of the alcove to where the two of them could be clearly seen from the main playground. 'Wha'?'

Ronnie looked around to check where Harding was – jogging safely from the ball by the school gate. He had stopped, and was staring at the two of them.

'I want to do this,' Ronnie said – and he suddenly plonked a kiss on Wendy's cheek. Her eyes rolled and she turned her head away in surprise.

'Cheeky mullock!' she said with hot eyes and a fierce frown – as Jack Harding came pelting across the playground faster than the bulleting ball.

'You! Bunny! I tol' ye...'

'Told me what?' Ronnie turned to face

the angry boy, squaring up, his fists clenched.

'Leave her alone!'

'You wanna fight?' Ronnie asked him. 'You wanna teach me what I can an' can't do?'

Jack Harding took a step back. The skipping rope was still. Wendy and all the girls were watching and listening.

'Ye're on!'

'Right. Put up your dukes.' Ronnie raised his fists and set his feet, right in front of left, turning his body sideways on. This was how his dad had taught him to fight, both of them being left-handed: to lead with his right and follow through with his left. And straight away this stance put off the right-handed Harding, because both their leading hands were on the same side. 'Touch, an' off,' Ronnie said.

Buzz-ball was suddenly dead as boys came crowding round, and the first shouts of 'Fight! Fight! Fight!' hit the air.

The two of them stared into each other's eyes, putting their leading fists forward for the touch before the punching began. There would be no feet, no wrestling, no dirty tricks. A fair fight was a fair fight.

Crack! Ronnie smashed his left hand into Jack Harding's cheek, who clearly didn't know how to defend against a cack-hander. But he rode it well, skipped back on light feet and came forward himself, looking to get one in on Ronnie's head.

But Ronnie's dad had taught him well. 'Most kids go for the head, always the head,' he'd say, 'so mix it – get in under his guard and give him one in the bread-basket...' Which is what Ronnie did. While three of their fists were at head height, Ronnie's left cracked in under Harding's right elbow and caught him hard in the stomach.

'Ooof!' said Harding. 'Low – tha's low.'

'Weren't.' Ronnie danced back. 'Above the belt.'

'Fight! Fight! Fight!' the cry went on, the two of them ringed in. The shouts were all for 'Jack! Jack! Jack!' with Wendy standing silent, eyes wide one moment, wincing the next as a punch landed. This was Jack Harding's on Ronnie's nose, who hadn't got back fast enough from a flailing fist. *Oh, that hurt!* His dad would have been ashamed of him, too pleased with his solar plexus blow to think about defence.

Ronnie was bleeding, and looked the worse of the two – but he reckoned Jack Harding was hurt more. He was doubled over, gasping for breath. Ronnie stepped in, pulled back his left arm for a knock-out punch into Jack Harding's face. But suddenly his arm couldn't move. His wrist was held in a fierce grip. And he realised that the shouting had stopped. The ring of spectators had blown away like smoke in the wind.

'Stow that right now!' It was Mr Bennett, the headmaster, who had come out from his office. A small man in a dark suit, watch and fob across his waistcoat, he still had the look of a handy lightweight. 'Inside!' he commanded. 'Inside, the two o' ye! I'll show ye some action.'

✗✗✗

The head's office was up a turn of stairs – small, tidy, spiralled with the smoke coming from a pipe of Digger Plug smouldering in an ashtray

'What a display! A war's on, an' we're fightin' among us-selves. Well, I c'n do some fightin' meself – to maintain order in the ranks.' His jacket was already off and he was rolling up his shirt-sleeves, reaching for the cane that was hanging on the radiator.

Ronnie dug into his pocket for a handkerchief, to dab at his nose. There was blood, but his nose wasn't streaming. His face was buzzing. Next to him Jack Harding was still trying to straighten up from the punch to his midriff. He'd been hurt badly.

'Right!' Mr Bennett swiped the cane down on to the desk and reached on the shelf behind him for the punishment book. He unscrewed the cap of his pen, but before he entered the date and the first name, he looked up and demanded, 'Who started it?' He looked from one to the other. 'Which of ye?'

Jack Harding had started it, Ronnie reckoned, by calling him 'Bunny'. But it had also been Smeaton and the rest who weren't going to let him fit into the school.

He looked at Harding. The boy was suffering, needed first aid. The solar plexus punch had been a beaut! Ronnie thought of his dad. Reg Warren always stood his ground, always came out clear against some of the things Uncle Len went on about, paid the rent regularly, and had never smacked Ronnie in anger. He was a man, his dad, and seeing the real pain and distress he'd given Harding, Ronnie suddenly decided that there was no option but to be a man, too.

He stepped forward, his nose held up to stop the bleeding. 'I started it, sir.'

Jack Harding turned to look at him. His face was the colour of fly-paper.

'You started it, did ye, lad? Ye come up from t' south to what succour we c'n give you, we fit you into an overcrowded class – which ye repay by starting trouble in playground. What sort of behaviour is that?'

Ronnie said nothing.

'Eh? Put a word to it.'

'Ungrateful, sir.'

Jack Harding was frowning at Ronnie as if he just couldn't understand what was going on.

'Right. Then you, Harding, you learn to keep your cool, an' when there's trouble, what do ye do?'

'Report it, sir.'

'Aye – report it to the teacher on duty. Tha's why I send staff outside in all weathers, for just that purpose.'

'Yes, sir.'

'Then ye stand aside.' Mr Bennett bent back to the punishment book. 'Name?' he demanded of Ronnie.

'Ronald Warren, sir.' As he gave it, Ronnie turned to look at Harding, to see if there was a hint of a silent 'Bunny' on his lips. But there wasn't. He was standing staring, with a hand still on his stomach and bewilderment in his eyes.

'It should be six,' Mr Bennett said. 'But ye stepped forward, so it'll be four.' He wrote the figure four beneath a line of sixes, capped his pen and picked up the cane, giving it a short cut in the air.

'Yes, sir,' Ronnie croaked.

The head stepped back to give himself room for the swing. Ronnie knew the drill. He hadn't been caned often, but he was no stranger to the stick. He raised his right hand, arm extended, his fingers as far back as he could get them because a caning on a cupped hand always hurt more. Mr Bennett took a sighting; and, as expected, Ronnie's hand was tapped by the cane from underneath to raise it to a good height for the stroke. He held his breath, waited – but he wasn't going to shut his eyes. He braced himself for what was coming.

One. The cane came down with a violent hiss, square across his palm. *Aaaaah! That hurt!* But he somehow kept his mouth shut as the sharp, brutal pain burned his hand – although what pricked his eyes was the shock of this assault on his body. Abjectly sorry for himself, he took in a huge breath.

'Position!' Mr Bennett commanded, and tapped up the raw hand to take the second cut. This time Ronnie shut his eyes – to keep the tears in. And, *two!* For the second stroke Bennett was off-target and swiped the stick across Ronnie's fingers instead of his palm – and Ronnie couldn't help it. *'Ow!'* he shouted, curling, then sucking them.

'Don't move next time. Left hand.'

Ronnie's heart was thumping hard inside his chest, and his mouth was filled with the bile of pain and hatred. But he somehow held himself steady, and shifted his feet as he held out his left hand. His right hand no longer belonged to him, hanging hot and withered at his side, while his body shook with the trauma of the punishment. *God, that hurt: this man knows how to dish it.* Ronnie took a look along his arm at his trembling left hand, which in a second or so would be as hurting and injured as the other.

Bennett grunted as he tapped him up again and lifted the cane high behind his shoulder. This was it again! This was going to—

Three. The worst – *Mum! Dad!* He'd taken this one from Bennett's better side, a right cut on a left hand. But against everything, his legs shaking now in pain and anticipation, Ronnie kept his mouth so tight shut that his teeth hurt, keeping his left arm out for the next, to get it over so that he could run to the lavatories and cry. But there was no way that Bennett was going to call him a southern coward.

'Put your arm down.'

What was this? Did they do the last one on the bum, up north?

'Get off to your class. Three'll do. Ye're a London lad who's taken stick off Adolf Hitler. Get to the cloakroom and sort out your nose – and think twice, lad, about ever again starting a fight in my school.'

'Yes … sir.' Ronnie's voice was shaking with his body; but he held himself to attention, in case Mr Bennett changed his mind about number four. His left hand hurt twice as much as his right.

The head re-lit his pipe as he dismissed Jack Harding, leaving the pair of them to squeeze through the door and out on to the small landing.

'C'n you throw a ball wi' that hand?' Harding asked, as they went down the stairs.

'I reckon so.' Ronnie might not be able to write on the lines in his exercise book at the next lesson, but Bennett's stick was not going to stop him throwing a ball.

'Ye're in for buzz-ball, then, dinner time.' And Harding found the wind to cuff Ronnie round the back of the head. 'Ye're in wi' lads now.'

Chapter Five

Around six o'clock each day, Auntie Barton geared the household to Eric coming home from his job at the railway offices. The big mill-worker woman made sure the table in the dining-room was ready laid, and no one was allowed to disturb a knife or a fork by a fraction of an inch – let alone snag the tablecloth and pull everything askew. After his first weekend, Ronnie was allowed to read in an armchair in the chilly front room – mostly the Robin Hood magazines his mother was sending him. It was better to go outside, and after the caning there were children in the street who would play with him. A boy called Roy Moor lived up the road, who'd sometimes knock at the door with a couple of others for a game of football between lampposts.

There was no question of them coming into the house – 'Them trouble ain't comin' in. Ye keep the street out in the street' – but on wet nights – and there were loads of those – Ronnie was allowed to swap comics on the front door mat.

Auntie Barton never had a smile for Ronnie, but a soppy look always came on her face when Eric's key scraped into the lock. It was enough to make the junket run. And Eric lived up to it. He'd sometimes bring in an evening paper – kept it crisp for her, never read it himself, but sported it under his arm, like a man in from business, as if he ran the railway. All he needed was a bowler hat.

Ronnie's Robin Hood stories were in books with paper covers, like magazines, but smaller. The print was in two columns down each page; but never mind what they were called, to him they were just 'my Robin Hoods'. A fresh one arrived every week, on a Wednesday or a Thursday morning, sent rolled-up with a letter from his mum wrapped inside the middle pages. And so avidly did he read them, that he was waiting for the next adventure a couple of days before it came. They were great stories – and he was Robin Hood, wasn't he? He, Ronnie Warren, had been sent away from London just as Robin had been from his Loxley homelands; and in the same way that Robin had arch-enemies in King John and the Sheriff of Nottingham, Ronnie had Adolf Hitler and fat Herman Goering, whose planes bombed London every night. The covers and the titles never failed to give him a lift as he undid the packages – although, strangely, Eric never wanted to borrow one. Perhaps he thought he was too grown up – but that pleased Ronnie, because Eric might take one to his office to read at dinner time, and Ronnie was collecting them. They were numbered.

Reading wasn't always easy, though. Some of the characters had difficult names, like the one Ronnie passed over as 'Guy-de-Goosegogs'. And the writers didn't mind slinging in a few historical words for parts of castles and for fighting weapons. These Ronnie blinked at and passed over as he read.

The big shock came one Saturday afternoon when he was in the front room reading 'Robin and the Arrows of Victory'. Eric was by the window where you could get the best wireless signal, listening to the Light Programme giving out scores from the wartime football league. It didn't interest Ronnie; it was all up-north stuff because the clubs weren't allowed to travel more than fifty miles from home, so Charlton wasn't in it. Sprawled on the settee, he came across a word he couldn't understand – which he really needed to know. *What was it?* Ronnie felt a real dope not knowing what the word meant. It was one he couldn't blink on or 'Goosegog' over because it came at the end of the sentence and he had to know it to follow the story: he had to know the something that Robin suddenly needed in order to look as if he was a sentry in the castle – but Ronnie had never heard of it.

All at once Robin realised that if he was to get into the castle and mingle with the guards he needed a coif. Without one he would be exposed, but with one he would not stand out. Where, though, in the humble villages near Sherwood, would the brave outlaw find himself a coif?

A coif? What the devil was a coif? Was it big, was it small, did it hang on a belt, did you wear it like clothes, or did you ride on it? Ronnie needed to know, if he was going to be Robin Hood in his head and think what he might do. Running the words of the last sentence over in his mind, he ducked across the room to Eric and the glowing wireless set.

'Here, Eric, what's Robin after here?' He held out the page with his thumbnail marking the mystery word.

Eric immediately waved him away as if he carried the plague. 'L-listening to f-football scores,' he said; and he put his ear as close to the wireless as a deaf granddad.

Ronnie went back to the settee, but through the next two columns of reading nothing made sense without knowing the meaning of that word 'coif'. Keeping a finger in the page, he waited for the football news to end, and then he slid across to Eric again.

'Eric – this word. You ever heard of one of whatever this is?'

'No, I ain't. I'm b-busy. Ask me m-mum.'

'She's out. Go on, just have a decko, won't take a sec...'

'T-told ye – I'm b-b-busy.' Eric was up and heading for the door, but Ronnie knew he wasn't busy. He'd already said how boring Saturdays were when North End was playing away.

'See – this one.' With his thumbnail and finger again bracketing the word, Ronnie stopped Eric and held the page up in front of his face, between him and the door. 'Have a quick look.'

'Not got t-time,' Eric said, back-handing the book aside.

'It's easy to read,' Ronnie pleaded. 'I just don't know how to say it or what it is.'

Eric suddenly turned and pushed his pimply face into Ronnie's. 'You s-sayin' I can't read,' he demanded, 'ye little c-c-c-clever-clogs? Jus' 'cos I ain't g-got the time to b-bother wi' your b-b-b-book...' It was a struggle to say, and with a push and a slam Eric was out of the room and swearing in the hallway.

Like a dowse of cold water, Ronnie knew: Eric *couldn't* read – at least, not well enough to be asked about a difficult word. This didn't bother Ronnie, but it was a surprise; although he quickly came to wondering how Eric Barton could be a clerk on the railway if he couldn't read and write properly. And, come to think of it, with all his collar studs and his cufflinks, Eric never had a pencil or a pen about his person, did he?

✕✕✕

Jack Harding would never be a best mate, but he was OK these days, and now that he'd gone off Wendy Penworth, he didn't mind Ronnie talking to her.

At playtime one afternoon, when the buzz-ball had gone over into the street and been squashed by a lorry, Ronnie ran to the alcove where she was skipping with the girls, and without asking permission he waited until her turn came, and ran into the rope with her.

Cinderella, dressed in yella
went upstairs to kiss a fella.
Made a mistake,
kissed a snake.
How many doctors did it take?
One, two, three, four...

And on they jumped until the count got to twenty – when Ronnie left one of his feet a bit too low.

Out!

But the other boys had arrived, and for five minutes the rope was a line of mixed boys and girls – including big-boy Derek Smeaton, who ran out of the rope at the wrong time and took it with him across his fat stomach. Now the argument started, and over came the teacher on duty to sort the commotion. Mr Kirkham.

'Wha's all this? Wha' you lads doin' in alcove?

Get out into yard.'

At that same moment Wendy pulled the rope away from Smeaton and waved it round and round in triumph, accidentally whipping the teacher across the face with it.

'Wha' the—!'

It must have hurt. Wendy couldn't have realised how close she was to the man, because the force of it closed one eye, and already he was marked across the cheek with a red weal.

Mr Kirkham turned. He stared. He glared anger and hate at Wendy. 'Blast ye!' he shouted. He suddenly grabbed at her, clutching a pigtail, and in a fit of spite he yanked and yanked and yanked.

'Ow! Ow! Ow!'

He jerked Wendy's head lower and lower towards the ground, taking it out on her.

'Ye stupid little cow!' And he wouldn't let go. As Wendy desperately clutched at his hand, he kept hold of the pigtail and pulled her head from side to side, twisting her neck this way and that. 'Ye knew... what... ye... was... doin'!'

'Stop it! I never!' Wendy was crying, screaming now in desperate pain.

Ronnie saw red. His guts electric, he ran face

to face with Mr Kirkham. He was Robin Hood confronting a scurvy varlet who was assaulting the lady Marion.

'Let her go!'

'Wha'? Will I—?' And with one eye staring like a madman, Kirkham jerked Wendy even harder, twisting and tugging at her pigtail with such force that it looked as though the screaming girl's neck would be seriously injured. 'Not till I've taught this little—'

Ronnie hit him. With a straight left-hander to make Reg Warren proud, he smashed his fist into the teacher's nose.

'You great bully!' he shouted at him. 'You spiteful swine!'

Kirkham staggered back and crumpled. Wendy dropped down to a crouch, shaking and sobbing. Ronnie stood there with his fist still clenched and ready.

'Run! Run! Run home!' Roy Moor shouted – as the headmaster came striding across the playground.

But Ronnie stood his ground. 'I'm not running nowhere!' – although he knew that hitting a teacher would get him ten of the worst and expulsion to Approved School. He pointed at Kirkham. 'That man's not fit to be here!'

At the sight of Mr Bennett the crowd dispersed, all but Wendy and Ronnie – and Jack Harding.

Kirkham's nose was broken, that was clear. His face was wonky, and blood puddled the playground. 'Warren!' the man finally managed to get out, and he pointed to his nose.

'Get yourself some first aid. Then take a bus down to the Royal Infirmary. I'll split your class,' the headmaster told him.

He turned to the three others: Wendy leaning against the wall, swollen-eyed, still racked with sobs; Ronnie standing to an attention as stiff as ever his dad would have done; and Jack Harding hovering there beside them. 'The three o' ye – upstairs.'

So Ronnie took a short walk towards his fate, twenty-five slow yards across the drizzly Lancashire playground.

Chapter Six

Jack Harding did most of the talking. Wendy was allowed to sit down. A couple of times she took her hands from the side of her head which she was holding, and nodded. Ronnie stood to attention, trying not to look at the cane hanging on the radiator – but ready to correct Jack if he had to.

But Jack did him proud. 'It were Mr Kirkham – never seen nothin' like it.'

'What, exactly?' Mr Bennett was sitting making notes, his eyes darting between Wendy and Ronnie.

'She caught 'im wi' rope, accident, like – then he went mad. What 'e done was cruel, real cruel, even for him…'

'Describe it, lad.'

"E got 'old of 'er hair, an' pulled half 'er head off. Lost 'is rag, sir, totally lost it – even for him.'

'You said, "Even for him". Is he often … short?'

Jack frowned. 'You know 'im, sir. All the time sendin' for punishment book, an 'e's got his own stick…'

'They're all recorded, Harding. Every stroke.'

Mr Bennett looked up at Ronnie.

Four, thought Ronnie, *crossed out to three.* But how many would it be this time?

'That's just the stick, sir. There's the ruler, an' the slipper, an' the board rubber, an' his fists…'

'His fists?' But why didn't the headmaster look very surprised?

'He'll gi' ye one any time – between yer shoulders, when ye're linin' up wrong, or not sittin' straight…'

Mr Bennett coughed.

'An' if ye can't do summat – like t'kids at the front – he'll slap your face or knuckle the top of yer 'ead. If I told me mam, she'd be up here like one o'clock.'

The headmaster stared at Jack, then pushed his paper away, capped his fountain pen, and stood thinking.

Ronnie took a deep breath. This was it.

Now Bennett would stick like glue to Kirkham and teach him what happens to boys who hit teachers. Canes and teachers run schools, not kids with a good left.

Mr Bennett stared at each of the three in turn. 'I'm saying nowt about Mr Kirkham, right? You'll live, will ye?' he asked Wendy.

The red of her scalp still burned through the pigtail parting, but Wendy nodded.

'I'm grateful to you, Harding. But you keep your accusations to yeself, you understand? A bit *purple*, I think.'

Jack straightened. 'Yes, sir.'

'As for you, Warren – ye've got to learn that in an… *incident*… you come running to the office, ye get me? Ye don' go round tekin' law into ye'r own hands.'

Ronnie's heart raced as the headmaster's lawful hand moved towards the radiator and the cane. 'Yes, sir,' he muttered. But the man suddenly slapped his side instead.

'I doubt Mr Kirkham's going to bring any charges – if Wendy's mam doesn't. Right, the three of you – back to class, an' see if you can get some education inside you…'

And that was it. *Off the hook* – leaving Wendy to go down the office stairs with Ronnie on one side and Jack on the other; but holding on to Ronnie's arm.

✗✗✗

Mr Kirkham didn't come back. Instead, a Mrs Davies came out of retirement and the classroom was a lighter place – but meanwhile, Ronnie took into school for Jack some of his prized possessions – a chunky bundle of Robin Hood stories. 'Ta, mate – you're a pal,' he told him.

'Ye're all right yerself, Ron. Your dad a boxer?'

'Not a real one. What about your'n?'

'Ain't got one, not since Dunkirk.'

Ronnie left it at that. But he reckoned Jack's dad would have been a decent bloke; wouldn't have minded him fighting alongside Reg Warren.

✗✗✗

That Friday night, Ronnie went home to a big surprise. The headmaster had had a note put through Auntie Barton's door. She read it, and showed it to him.

It is my duty to inform you that during the week your evacuee Ronald Warren deemed it appropriate to assault a member of staff, causing damage to a bone in his nose. While there were special circumstances involved in the incident, Ronald must be made aware that a repetition of this sort of behaviour will incur the severest punishment. Etc., etc.

Ronnie had kept his punching quiet. Like rescuing his mother, it was something he was still too proud of to talk about. Now he told Auntie Barton the whole story. She listened in silence.

When Eric came in, Auntie Barton waved the letter at him and told him its contents.

'It were K-K-Kirkham?'

Ronnie nodded, and repeated the story for him.

'Yes!' Eric suddenly shouted. 'Yes! You done wha' had to be done. Top dog! Top dog! An' I owe you, Ron, I owe you.' For once, he hadn't stuttered, but although he couldn't keep it up, what he said next was as good as anyone could hope to hear. 'I t t tell ye what – I'm g-g-givin' ye t-t-top bunk, I am. Aye. Ye deserve it.' And hiding his face, he ran out of the kitchen.

Ronnie stared at Auntie Barton, and saw that she was crying.

'Kirkham was a pig,' she said, getting up and wiping her eyes on her apron. 'He did for our Eric, that man. When Eric picked up a pencil with his left hand, he'd hammer it wi' the ruler. When he couldn't read hard words he'd get cuffed round the head…'

Ronnie was silent, sitting on his own hands.

"E shot that boy's nerves. Give him the twitches an' the stammer.' She stood up. 'Looks like you broke the bugger's nose, lad. Well, I stopped Eric's dad doing it, but I'd still break the man's bloody neck tomorrow, I can tell you.'

She stopped in the doorway.

"Scusin' my French,' she said.

The
American
Captain

Chapter One

'I'm not losing two of you!'

Ronnie and his mother were on the country bus taking them from Braintree railway station to the village of Chalkney Green, out in Essex. Back in London the flying bombs were bringing their new and spooky danger from the air – but the explosion that had rocked the Warrens was the telegram from the War Office. Ronnie's dad had been posted 'Missing in action'.

Missing?

Ivy Warren had kept the small slip of tragic paper in her pocket until Ronnie came in from school. 'They don't say much on the telegram – although they don't definitely say that he's... ' She'd hardly been able to get the word out; it had come from so far down in her throat, '… Dead.'

'What *does* it say?' Exact words were very important. Were they the same as on Jack Harding's mother's telegram, back in Preston?

'Well. "Missing in action – presumed dead." Only *presumed*.' Her hand had gone to her Royal Artillery brooch, stroking it. 'Uncle Len told me if no one finds his identity disc they check the battlefield casualty stations, but if he's been picked up by the Germans, you have to wait till the Red Cross get into their hospitals and prisoner-of-war camps.'

Ronnie had said nothing. He just hadn't been able to think of his big, laughing, man of a dad as *dead*. And after a squeeze of his mother's hand, he'd gone into the kitchen to make her a cup of tea, running the hot water one-handed round the pot to warm it, the grown-up way his dad did.

xxx

It was the middle of July, 1944, and Uncle Len had gone on ahead to Essex. It was supposed to be secret, but because Uncle Len lodged with them, they knew about it. Some key Woolwich Arsenal workers had been drafted down to Shoeburyness to the gun ranges where they tested shells. And with the doodlebugs coming over day and night with no warning, Ronnie's mother decided they were going, too – because she wasn't going to have the Germans killing any more Warrens. Uncle Len's father lived in a cottage at Chalkney Green, where Uncle Len went at weekends, and there was a room for them there, if they shared.

Ronnie hated the idea of leaving London and his mates again. He'd come home from Preston when the Blitz petered out, and for three years life had been half normal – until the doodlebugs started droning over. He reckoned that if your name was on a bomb, your name was on a bomb – and he'd take his chances. But that terrible telegram had rocked his mum. She didn't limp any more, but what she called 'the stuffing' had been knocked out of her. And she'd decided that she wasn't going to lose Ronnie to a doodlebug hitting the school. They were going to stick together somewhere safe until the war as over. Her eyes seemed to have changed. Instead of being bright and alive they had gone dull, with a hollow look to them like someone staring into a dark pool. Her voice, too, was flatter, and when cheerful music came on the wireless she'd turn it off.

Ronnie tried to make up for it. He found things to do to help her, and he kissed her more than usual. And he told her whenever he could that his dad wasn't dead – he'd be too clever, he'd dodge a bullet and keep his head down when the shells came over. Ronnie believed all this. He was sure Dad was going to come home again one day.

'I can find work in Essex,' his mother told him as she got on with the packing. 'The Optical Buildings have had a word with the American Air Force – they've got bases nearby. Or I'll clean for people, or work on the land, if it comes to it...' Ronnie knew this was likely to happen. With her hair in a scarf and wearing her dungarees, she could roll up her sleeves with the best of them.

She could graft, his mum, however heavy her heart.

So that Saturday morning they travelled to Chalkney Green by train and country bus, to be met outside the Three Ashes by Uncle Len and his old dad.

It was like a different land. Out here, the countryside went on for miles and miles. The bus had brought them along lanes between fields and through woods and across a river. And everywhere was brightness. Ronnie found himself squinting, because every look upwards was filled with sky. And with no bombed shops or warehouses or churches, no signs anywhere of the war, it felt like being in a peacetime film.

This was the thought in his head as the bus turned a corner – and he suddenly ducked low in his seat when a great, low aircraft came roaring over them.

A woman across the aisle laughed. 'You'll get used to them round here. Yanks. *"Got any gum, chum?"'*

'American Air Force,' Ronnie's mum explained.

'Ah.' And from then on, Ronnie never quite lost that aircraft sound in his ears; it was the background to this part of the country.

✗✗✗

'Call me Uncle Will,' Uncle Len's dad said. He meant that for Ronnie's mum as well as for Ronnie. 'So you're Ronnie. And, o' course, you'll remember me, Ivy, from the wedding…'

Ronnie's mum nodded as if she did, but there

was no smile, because what he was doing now was telling her how sorry he was about Reg. The old man would have been tall, like Uncle Len if his top half hadn't been so bent over. His face, too, was in line with Uncle Len's, except that it was beardy, but not long and whiskery – more like someone who'd lost his razor for a couple of days. He wore big leather boots laced up to his ankles, and never mind the summer sun, he was wearing a cap and long tweed overcoat with a white silk scarf at his throat.

'C'mon.' He grabbed the suitcase and wouldn't let anyone take it from him. 'Nah! The day I can't carry a travellin' bag's the day I'm sleeping on the parlour table...'

Ronnie frowned. 'In his coffin,' Ivy whispered, as they followed along the village street – an image that was shot out of his head as another low aircraft suddenly came roaring over them, its undercarriage down and the rivets along its fuselage distinct enough to be counted. On the side and the wings was the star of the American air force.

'Marauder,' Uncle Len told him. 'Going in to Earls Colne.'

'Yankee bombers,' old Uncle Will said. 'Our British boys bomb at night an' these cowboys bomb in the day. You'll soon get used to it. They come over so low sometimes they'll take the top off your egg for you.'

'Egg?' said Ronnie's mum. Eggs were strictly rationed.

'Got me own chickens, girl. You won't go short of an egg or two down here...'

They walked past the village pond to the old man's cottage. 'Welcome to Greengates' – which happened to be painted brown – 'an' wipe your feet goin' in, boy.'

The bedroom Ronnie shared with his mum was at the back, looking out over a long garden shaped like a question mark – a bit like Uncle Will himself. The whole room was taken up by a single bed and a camp bed. And Ronnie wasn't all that delighted with the thatched roof that stretched down over the small window. Spiders and mice, that's what country thatch harboured, according to Uncle Len – and big, they were, Essex spiders; 'You could fry one for your supper.' The bedroom sloped, so from the door to the window you went downhill, and it was hard for Ronnie not to roll out of his camp bed. Uncle Will slept in the front bedroom, and now that they were here, Uncle Len shared the room with him at weekends, in his own camp bed under the window. 'Can't sleep downstairs,' he said, 'it's not natural. Need to go up the wooden hill to Bedfordshire...'

Ronnie disagreed. He'd sooner have gone down the concrete pit to his bunk in the shelter, thanks very much. The same went for the lavatory. In London they had a lav with water and a chain, even if it was out in the back garden, but here the place his uncles called 'the privy' was across a patch of baldy grass in a sort of log cabin. And, *phew*, the smell! as you went in – some sort of dark brown, Marmitey chemical that sucked in what you sent down. But the thing Ronnie disliked most of all was not having electricity, or even gas. They cooked on a wood stove, and for lighting they had paraffin lamps – which sent frightening shadows all over the stairs and the walls, leaving too many dark corners where anything could be lurking.

But it was great having an American bomber base just a few miles off. Ronnie could read the markings on the Marauders, which he soon started spotting like a reconnaissance man.

The main thing Ronnie and his mother looked out for was the post, because this was how the telegrams arrived out here. A telegram saying that his dad was taken prisoner, or dead, would come trundling down The Street on a cranking old bicycle ridden by Mrs Caldew who ran the Post Office shop, her long grey hair puffed out behind her like exhaust. Before school each day, Ronnie listened for that crank; but nothing much came to Greengates until their second week, when the postmistress knocked to give his mother a letter in a thick envelope – none of that flimsy War Standard stuff.

'Trust the Yanks, girl. Better everything, they've got – rations, uniforms, dollars, an' paper.' Mrs Caldew hovered as if she was waiting to help read the letter; but Ivy Warren thanked her and went inside.

Ronnie had to know what this American letter said. 'Not... anything...?' he asked.

'I've got work,' Ivy told him, her eyes a fraction brighter, 'over at Earls Colne, at the base...'

'The Yanks?'

'Americans. Call them Americans, Ron. I went for an interview while you were at school, and they've given me this job, on account of being from the Optical Buildings.'

'How do you mean?'

'It means I'm a safe pair of hands. The manager at the Optical Buildings suggested it – and the Americans have checked up on me...'

'I don't get you.' Ronnie would be late for school now – but he had to know. His mother wouldn't be flying over Germany, would she?

'It's only a job in the canteen on the base – but they know I'm not likely to be a spy.'

'Good for you.'

'Good for both of us. You get a few treats, and I get out of the cottage all day.' This would suit her, Ronnie knew. Uncle Will was all right, but he'd shown them already that he wasn't any more fun to be with than Uncle Len. Moaning came as naturally to him as growling does to a dog.

'When do you start?'

'Monday.'

'That's all right, then.'

She had perked up a bit. 'So get yourself off to school, and go like one o'clock or you'll be late,' – which Ronnie did; but he found the breath to whistle 'Yankee-doodle-dandy' on the way.

Chapter Two

But Monday didn't turn out to be at all wonderful. It was the beginning of mother-problems for Ronnie – and it was the day when he got tangled up with Evie Michaels.

Evie Michaels was fourteen, due to leave school at the same time as Ronnie at the end of the summer term; but she'd been absent since he'd come to Chalkney Green. 'Helping me mum with the picking,' she told the teacher – which was accepted without a fuss. And from his first sight of her, a nervous feeling trembled in Ronnie's guts. She and Ronnie were the only two of the same age in the school – the oldest in the class – so they were soon paired off for partner activities. This wouldn't have been a problem, if she hadn't treated him as if he was an infant.

'You talk up there,' she told him the first playtime, saying it in soprano. 'When's your voice gonna break?' She was carrying her side of the milk crate a foot higher than he was on his side. 'S'posed to break when you're fourteen, boy.'

'All in good time,' said Ronnie. This was one of his mum's sayings, but he said it as low as he could manage without coughing.

'You start to be a man, then.' Evie Michaels was more like a woman than a girl. She bobbed up and down inside her loose frock, and her legs had a dancer's shape to them.

Well, Ronnie was a man already, thanks. He was the man of the house, just as his dad had asked him to be. He'd saved his mum's life in an air raid and he'd broken the nose of a bully teacher and got to be top bunk up north. And now that he was fourteen, he was allowed to wear long trousers. What more was there to being a man than that?

'You like cherries?' They put down the crate and sorted the empty bottles.

'They're all right.'

'If you come round our place s'afternoon an' help pick the last of 'em, me mum'll give you some for your tea.'

Uncle Will had gooseberries and chickens in his long garden, and cabbages and spuds up at the back – but he didn't have cherries.

'Might do,' Ronnie said.

'Oh, I see,' Evie scorned – '*I'll have to ask me dad!*'

'My dad's gone missing,' Ronnie said.

'Run off?'

'Missing in the war.'

She didn't go into that. 'Up to you. I'll foot your ladder.'

'I'm not scared of heights.' To be honest, Ronnie wasn't sure this was true – which made things confusing when he found himself walking home with the girl, way over on the other side of the village; knowing in his heart that he was only going because he'd been scared not to.

Her place was a surprise. It was across a bridge on the other side of a fast stream, up a track behind a five-barred gate, which she was over like a vaulter. And where Uncle Bill's cottage was definitely in the country compared with London, it was still on The Street, with a tarred road in front of it; while Evie Michaels' place – what she called 'the holding' – was tucked away like a secret among trees and fields, with a big dog running at them, barking.

'He's all right,' Evie told Ronnie, sensing his London fear of dogs without collars. 'Let him get a sniff of you.' She held the dog's scruff while Ronnie stood to let the dog smell him. And where do dogs always have to smell you on a hot day? Always in an embarrassing place. 'Stand still – he won't bite it off.'

Ronnie felt bitten off already. However grown up he tried to think himself in his long trousers, whatever he did when he was with Evie made him feel small.

'What's your game?' Evie's mother wanted to know, looking at the pair of them. She was a big woman, obviously belonging to the same family as Evie. Her hair was done up in a style like something off a Roman statue; an apron covered her front, its floral design all spattered with juices, and she was in gum boots.

'He's gonna pick cherries. I said he could have some if he got enough down.'

'He don't look the country picking sort to me.' Evie's mother was frowning, looking Ronnie up and down worse than the sniffing dog. 'An't got the outside on his face at all.'

'Won't know till he tries, will he?' Evie persisted,

pushing on past her mother, taking Ronnie by the hand and dragging him towards their home. It wasn't a farmhouse or even a cottage, but an old railway carriage standing on wooden sleepers. Evie led him up a couple of steps and in through a door with a big '3' painted on it, and from the kitchen area she picked up a tablecloth and a wicker shopping basket. 'Here y'are. I'll take you over the orchard.'

Ronnie couldn't help stealing a quick look around. It didn't look like a train inside. All the partitions had gone, and there were a few chairs and a settee, making it look like a long, glorified caravan.

'C'mon – stop your gawping.' Evie pulled at his arm and shoved him out of the door, where the force of her had him jumping the steps. She tied a length of washing-line to the handle of the basket as they walked, and pulled him through a gap in a yew hedge to a small cherry orchard. By now the dog was following, and running towards them were a couple of infants Ronnie remembered seeing in the yard at the village school.

'Clear off – we're workin',' Evie told them. But they followed all the same.

Up close, the cherry trees looked big. The first in the line had been picked clean of fruit. The ladder stood propped among the leaves and branches of the second, but it wasn't that tall – it only reached a third of the tree height, with cherries growing above it all the way to the top.

'You go as high as you can on the ladder – then you climb in the branches. You can climb a tree, can't you?'

"Course I can.' But Ronnie wasn't so sure about these trees. He had a couple of climbing favourites on Plumstead Common whose handholds and footholds he knew – but they were plane trees, with thicker branches than this cherry tree.

'Up you go, then. I'll do this bottom lot from the ground.' Evie spread the tablecloth on the grass. 'When your basket's full, let it down by the rope.'

'OK.' Ronnie made the ladder as firm as he could against the trunk of the tree, and tried to look agile as he went up the first few rungs. But once his head was up into the leaves and twigs and cherries, he suddenly asked himself what the dickens he was doing up a tree on a hot afternoon, picking cherries for some girl and her mother. How come he'd been talked into this? He should be at the cottage, laying the table for his mum to get the tea. Or reading a copy of The Wizard out in the garden with a glass of cold water from Uncle Will's well.

'Get on, then.'

And long flannel trousers were hotter than he'd thought. When the big day had come for wearing them, a second-hand pair with turn-ups, he'd been delighted – but, to be honest, his old shorts would have been better for this sort of thing. Below him, Evie was picking fast, and he was still manoeuvring the basket to where he could pick and fill it. But after a few moments – and in the density of the foliage forgetting he was ten feet off the ground – he made a good start. Slipping his hands between the leaves, he grasped at cherries in their twos and dropped them into the basket. And it was satisfying seeing the basket filling, until without moving his position it was soon full and he shouted down, 'Basket's ready.'

"Bout time an' all. Let it down gentle.'

Carefully, Ronnie lowered the basket through the branches until Evie could take it – pulling the rope with it and almost yanking him off the ladder.

'Well done, boy,' she called up; and Ronnie felt a tingle of pride down the backs of his legs. 'Pull up.'

Ronnie now had a system. He didn't need to keep going down to the ground to shift the ladder; he could move like a monkey among the branches –

always one hand for your grip, the other for your job, as his dad used to tell him. Basket followed basket – until a sudden nervous pang told him enough was enough. He had to get home.

'Gotta finish now,' he shouted down, although he hadn't yet cleared the tree to the top. 'Didn't tell me mum I was coming here.' He expected an argument from Evie along the lines of was he man or mouse? but that didn't happen.

'Let's have that last basket, then you c'n fill your shirt for yourself...'

A couple of the fat, dark, cherries had gone down his shirt front already, but now that he knew what his reward would be, Ronnie picked himself a bulging shirt-full. Being late home would be forgiven when he walked in with his fruity wages, wouldn't it? And it hadn't been so bad. When he saw Evie's tablecloth heaped with cherries, he felt proud of his work; a pride swollen by the skill he'd discovered high off the ground up that tree. He'd willingly come back and do some more tomorrow.

'Ta, boy. You didn't do so bad.' And Evie grabbed his shoulders and kissed him on the cheek.

A kiss from this girl who scared and excited him was something to remember. Clutching his shirt-full of cherries, he walked across the orchard towards the gap in the hedge, thrilled at her touch, and aware that she'd be standing watching him – and, still tingling, he accidentally stepped his right foot into his left trouser turn-up and fell flat on his stomach on the ground.

Behind him, Evie yelled with laughter, and dog and children all came running to look.

So much for feeling proud of himself! So much for cherries for tea. So much for a white school shirt. And so much for stupid long trousers...

Chapter Three

Ronnie's mum came home in a jeep. At twenty past six the canvas-topped American Air Force vehicle pulled up outside Greengates – a sight that took Uncle Will's eyes off watching Ronnie trying to wash his shirt.

'Oil me ticker,' the old man said, his hand on his heart, 'what've we got here?' But before he could get to the cottage door, Ronnie's mum had walked round the back and into the kitchen. 'You come home by *transport*?' he asked.

'I did!' To Ronnie she suddenly sounded like his mother from the time before that telegram had come. 'The captain goes into Braintree, so he gave me a lift.'

'Chalkney Green ain't on the way to Braintree from Earls Colne…'

'Isn't it? Haven't got my bearings yet.' She turned to Ronnie, who had vigorously resumed his washing. 'What are you doing, Ron?'

But it was Uncle Will who answered. 'Bit o' dhobying. Been scrumping. Fell over wi' a shirt full of cherries.'

'Ronnie! I'll never get that out.'

'It stains worse'n sin, the cherry.'

Ronnie could do without the old man sticking his oar in. 'I wasn't scrumping. I was asked. This person at school… this girl… she asked me to help pick some cherries for her mum, and she let me bring some home.'

'Only he never. Went bum over bonce on 'em instead.'

'Aaah… Trying to be helpful.' His mother scruffed Ronnie's hair.

'He never told me about no girl,' Uncle Will went on. 'Just said he'd been up a tree at the cherries.'

Shut up, Uncle Will! Hadn't the old goat got things to do, like emptying the chemical pan out the back? Ronnie was thinking that half the trouble with the war was having to live his own life all mixed up with other people's.

But Uncle Will wasn't budging. 'What's the truth of it, then?' he asked, as if he was Ronnie's dad.

Ronnie sensed his mother getting tight inside – that feeling of being about to say something you're going to wish you hadn't. She looked tired, but still smart in her summer dress and leather shoulder bag, her hair curled for work; and he'd have much rather she told him about her first day at the American base rather than him having to explain his accident. So he jumped in.

'I'm not lying. I didn't not tell him. I just didn't tell him everything, till you got home,' – meaning that his shirt was their business, not the old man's. 'It's boring...'

'Finding money an' coupons for new shirts an't boring, boy.'

The old fool wasn't going to back off. For two pins, Ronnie would have scooped up a pan of washing water and poured it over his head, cap and all. '...This girl at school lives over the bridge. In a railway carriage place that's got cherry trees in a field. I helped pick some cherries for her and her mum. That's all.'

'Very ki... ' Ronnie's mum began.

'Railway carriage? What's her name?' Uncle Will demanded. All at once he seemed to have straightened out of his stoop.

'She's called Evie...'

'Evie *what*?' The old man banged the kitchen table, and Ronnie's mum span round at him.

'Michaels,' Ronnie said. 'Evie Michaels.'

'Hah!' Uncle Will sat down; then stood up, his face a caricature of disgust. 'It's not *Michaels*,' he told them with spit on his lips. 'They changed it. It's *Micheli*. Mich-eli. The man's an Eyetie. Italian. They took him off an' shut him up somewhere, soon as the war kicked off.'

'Interned...?' Ivy Warren queried.

'An' I tell you both – I don' want no one living in this house associating with no Eye-talians.' He glared at the pair of them. 'I mean that.' He suddenly grabbed his coat from its hook. 'Gawd help us! I'm up the Ashes,' he said. 'You've shamed me, boy – shamed me.' And his slam of the kitchen door must have brought a few spiders and mice down from the thatched roof.

✗✗✗

They walked out to a field at the back, somewhere away from the cottage and from any eyes at the windows of the Three Ashes. Two horses stood in the far corner – biggish animals that Ronnie was a bit nervous about – which went back to their grazing as Ronnie and his mother sat themselves under a sycamore tree.

'Stupid old man!' she said. 'Going off like a doodlebug over Italians. They're allies now. On our side. They switched over – and the Germans killed thousands of them. They're fighting for us...'

'So why doesn't her dad come home? That girl's?' Ronnie was oddly shy about saying Evie's name.

His mother shrugged. 'They sent some of them to Canada. Probably won't get back till the war's over.' She took in a deep breath. 'Oh, I don't know what I'm going to do. I'm bloomin' pleased to keep out of the old fool's way most of the week.'

And now he was going to do the same, Ronnie thought: he'd stay out after school every afternoon until his mum came home from the base.

'It was hard work today, Ron,' his mother told him, standing up and brushing grass off the back of her frock. 'Getting used to the routine and having things ready for when the guys came back off ops.'

Guys! She was starting to talk American already. 'Like a café, is it?'

'Restaurant, hamburger bar, from steaks down to pretzels...'

'Pretzels?'

'Their sort-of crisp things. They buy them to take up on the raids.'

This was exciting. Ronnie could easily picture the Americans up in the air in their goggles and flying suits – pilots and gunners and bomb-aimers and navigators – dodging bullets and hoping they didn't have to bale out on their parachutes, crunching pretzels they'd got from his mother.

'You talk to Marauder pilots? Squadron leaders?'

'Majors. They call their squadron leaders "majors".'

'Ah.' She was really getting into this American flying stuff. 'Was that a major who brought you home?' he asked.

'Who gave me a lift on his way to Braintree? No.' She pulled Ronnie up and started walking back towards the cottage. 'He's a captain – that's below a major, like one of our flight lieutenants – on the ground, one of those admin men who run the station.'

'Didn't see him.' But what Ronnie suddenly did see were the two horses ahead – they'd crossed the field and stood between them and the track to the cottage. He hung back, while his mother went marching on – so he ran to catch up. If she could be brave with horses, so could he!

'What's his name?' he asked, trying to sound confident. 'The captain who drove the jeep?'

'Good boy. But I've got nothing for you.' Ronnie watched as his mother stroked the first horse's nose. She did the same to the second. 'Out of the way now – we've got tea to put on the table.'

And on she walked, not answering Ronnie's question. She probably hadn't heard him.

✕✕✕

Ronnie's mum put aside his stained shirt to cut up for rags, and found him a grey one for the next day. Like everyone else, they'd had their dinner at midday, Ronnie at school and his mum at the base. Tea was usually something on bread or toast, and tonight it was dripping; and for afters they had an apple each, a Granny Smith from Uncle Will's tree. But there wasn't much talk sitting up at the table. It seemed they both had things on their minds.

For Ronnie, it was Evie Michaels and what he was going to do about her. It was still a warm evening, and after helping with the cups and plates he went outside and lost himself over beyond the pond at the edge of a field of corn. Uncle Len had shown them the crops on their first Sunday: the fields of cabbages, the potatoes and these acres of corn. Ronnie ate cornflakes, and he knew how bread was made – but he was impressed to see the corn growing out of the ground and not in a loaf or a packet in a London shop.

He sat at the field's edge, cross-legged in his after-school shorts, and watched the corn swaying in the breeze, all the stalks going together, putting him in mind of a football crowd heading for the gates after a Charlton match. But he decided he wouldn't touch a husk of it. Food was precious. Ships got sunk bringing this sort of thing into the docks, so he wouldn't nibble even a grain to see what it tasted like. The big thing really worrying him was Uncle Will's command that he mustn't have anything to do with Evie. If he did, Uncle Will would find out and they couldn't live down here any more – they'd have to go back to London and the doodlebugs. Ronnie knew his mother wouldn't want that. He wouldn't mind, but then, he hadn't been bombed-on like her, had he? It was going to be awkward, though, keeping himself to himself with Evie. They were partners for work, and they were milk and ink monitors – they did those jobs together. So it was going to be hard being friendly with her in school – and having nothing to do with her after home time.

But this wasn't the whole of it, by a long way. The truth was, he liked Evie a lot. She'd stuck up for him in front of her mother, and she'd treated him like a real country boy after he'd got all those cherries down. And there was something about her that made him want her to like him. She put him in mind of Jane Russell, the film star in *The Outlaw,* the big film he'd seen not so long ago. When she was on the screen you couldn't take your eyes off her – and it wasn't just that she was beautiful, it was her the way she looked at you – the way Evie did. Jane Russell had fizzed Ronnie like sherbet at the pictures, and now the same thing had happened with this Italian girl down here in the country.

Here, on the edge of a peaceful corn field, he was grinding his teeth and digging his nails into the palms of his hands: hating Uncle Will for having his head stuck in the Marmite over Italians, trying to sit on an anger inside that was all mixed up with the fizz of Evie Michaels, and a guilty feeling for having the fizz in the first place. His mother had said, 'I don't know what I'm going to do.' Well, he didn't, either.

Why couldn't life be like it was before he went into long trousers?

Chapter Four

She came home in the same jeep again – and this time Ronnie met the captain. He knew it was the same jeep because the last three digits of the serial number along the bonnet were '127', the number of their house in Plumstead. So was this going to be a regular lift home from work? Perhaps the captain had to go to Braintree every evening. Ronnie went round the side of the cottage and in through the back door; but no one was in there. The voices were coming from the front room.

'Are you sure you won't have a cup of anything? Tea, coffee…?' This was Ronnie's mother.

'I don't want to be rude, ma'am, but no, thank you kindly.'

'I know our coffee's out of a bottle, but the tea's OK.'

'I'll be getting back to my place...'

Ronnie looked through the crack in the door before he went in. The American captain was tall, and with his smart black moustache he looked like the film star Gary Cooper. His uniform was sharp and smooth, not like Ronnie's dad's rough army battledress.

He turned and saw Ronnie. 'Hey, you must be Ronnie...'

'It certainly is.' Ronnie's mother smiled. 'He's fourteen, and tall for his age, isn't he?'

'Tall an' handsome.'

'He leaves school at the end of the summer...'

'Is that so?'

The captain addressed Ronnie. 'You don't plan on going to High School, then?'

'High School don't figure on having him...' Ronnie's mother was sounding more American by the day.

'Well, I guess I'll see you tomorrow, Ivy...' The captain pulled his brown leather gloves from under his epaulettes.

'God willing, and no stray doodlebugs.'

'Sure.' He looked for a second as if he might kiss her on the cheek. But he didn't, he put a hand on her shoulder instead. 'By the way, I'm Clay Miller,' he told Ronnie, and offered him his hand. Ronnie took it. It was much smoother than his mother's lens-grinding hands. 'I'll be seeing you, son.'

Ronnie nodded, but he didn't walk out of the room. For some reason he wanted to be there until the captain went. And when the captain did go, and the jeep drove off kicking up the dust, Ronnie noticed that his mother's eyes looked more normal than they had for a long while. His own, though, were dimmed by frowning over how to deal with the Evie Michaels business; and something else, too, that he couldn't get a handle on.

✗✗✗

The bus went through the village at a quarter to eight in the morning, and Ivy Warren had to be on it. But there was no way Ronnie wanted to stay in the cottage with Uncle Will until school time. The next day he was up early and dressed for school by the time his mother was ready to walk along to the bus stop at the Three Ashes.

Ronnie had rucked up his bed the night before, tormented by having to choose between either treating Evie as nobody special in school that day, or leaving things just the way they were before, him letting her give him a kiss on the cheek, then explaining later why he couldn't go home with her. But Evie didn't come to school that day. And school was *nothing* without her. There was nothing to make him fizz. Missing someone special leaves you flat, and he knew that even a cherry after school wouldn't have tasted the same.

Things went well with Uncle Will, though. Because Ronnie had gone straight home – which meant he wasn't with Evie – the old man shook his hand as he came through the back door. He mixed Ronnie a glass of his home-made ginger beer, but as soon as he'd drunk it, Ronnie told him he was going for a walk – along the path by the corn fields and through the lanes up towards the American base.

'I'm going to get a look at the Marauders on the ground.'

'You might meet your mum coming out – but don't get shot at by a Yankee sentry.'

Upstairs getting changed, Ronnie could see in the dressing table mirror that he was starting to tan –

getting the outside on his face, as Evie's mother called it. Now he needed his legs to lose their London whiteness. He found his shorts, swapped his shoes for a pair of sandals – no socks – and put on an old shirt with short sleeves. Why he'd want to do this to go up to the airfield, he didn't know – but it was a hot afternoon.

'What's the best way?' he asked Uncle Will, who was outside the back door sharpening a billhook with a stone.

'You go round Baxter's fields, jump the stream, up the Coggeshall road, along the Earls Colne road, an' you're all but there.'

'What stream?'

'Runs into the river – ain't wide enough to trouble a lad like you. Used to dam it up as boys, some of us. An' keep whistling – bit of a lovers' lane, that shady bank.'

But Ronnie could never imagine Uncle Will as a boy. He was one of those people who'd always been an old man – like Uncle Len. He left him swiping his billhook and headed off for Baxter's cornfields.

It was a lovely afternoon. It put Ronnie in mind of bike rides with his dad, out of London and over

Dartford Heath. Not many birds were singing – the planes had probably scared them all off – but the hedges buzzed, and the sun felt like warm ointment on his face. It was so pleasant, in fact, that when he had the choice of going through a shady copse that bordered the stream, or keeping the sun on his face, he chose the warmth.

And by some mystery of life, he found himself at Evie's place.

'Well, I'll be blowed,' he said aloud, almost as if Uncle Will could hear – because inside, deep down, he somehow wasn't a bit surprised.

And there she was, sitting on the steps of the railway carriage peeling potatoes. She looked up, but said nothing; didn't smile, didn't beckon him on or shoo him away. He could hear the dog and the kids somewhere over the back; but she was on her own. He stood with his weight on one foot ready to turn and go, if that was the way she wanted it...

'Come on, then. Don' be shy. You're looking more the country boy s'afternoon.' It was Evie's mother, who'd come round the back of the railway carriage carrying an armful of dried washing.

Ronnie didn't know whether to go on or go back. But even when she was ignoring him, Evie Michaels was a weird sort of magnet. Her mother went into the carriage – and he walked over to her.

'You wasn't at school today,' he said, stating the obvious.

'Miss me, did you?' She looked up at him.

Yes, he had. But he shook his head. 'Not much. Managed the milk crate all right.'

'Kept your ink spout steady, did you?' She suddenly threw the potato knife at the ground, sticking it upright. She stood, looked him in the eyes. 'We've heard about my dad,' she said.

'What've you heard?' Ronnie wasn't sure that he wanted to know. Dealing with someone else's misery was a misery in itself.

She took his hand, hers still wet from the potato water, and led him down past the end of the railway carriage to a long seat in the sun, set like something on a station platform. But she said nothing for ages. He could smell the peeled potatoes on her hands, but also feel the warmth of her body. And he couldn't help it: he put his arm around her shoulders. Poor kid, had she heard the something terrible?

'It's not bad news,' she said, although she didn't pull away. 'Not all bad.' Her hair tickled his cheek, her hand rested on his knee, and he fizzed.

He fizzed – which he shouldn't have been doing.

'How d'you mean?'

'My dad was sent to work in Canada, an' he had a farming accident in Canada. Went under a tractor…'

'Oh – that's rotten.'

'But they saved his life. He's lost a leg, and he's not well up here.' Evie tapped Ronnie's forehead. 'But he's alive.'

'That's smashing. That's really smashing.' Ronnie would settle for that – his dad with one leg and shell-shocked – if he was still alive.

'I thought he wasn't.' Her voice was down in her throat, deeper than Ronnie could ever manage, but quiet. 'When you don't get no letters, you think they're dead, or they've fell in with someone else…'

'I don't. I know my dad's still alive somewhere…'

Ronnie's arm was still around her, her hand was still on his knee, and it wasn't her hair touching his face now but her cheek, warm against his. 'Is that why you never came to school?'

'We had to go to London to look at his photo. He looks ninety-nine, Ron.'

Ron! He fizzed again. Only his mum ever called

him Ron. It was an in-the-house thing – and it sounded terrific coming from Evie.

But thoughts of in-the-house cooled him. He'd better get back before Uncle Will got nosy. He took his arm from around her shoulders and stood up. 'I've gotta go. I was supposed to be... ' But he didn't know what he was supposed to be doing; he dreaded getting back to the cottage; he wasn't going to be very good at secret stuff.

She laughed at him. 'You don't like those high trees, do you?' she mocked.

'That's it,' he said. 'Yeah, that's it. I'll see you.'

'Not if I see you first!'

This, he knew, was only a joke – and he wished like hell he didn't have the guilty feeling that came with nice things like that.

xxx

He ran round the pond into The Street and saw the jeep outside the cottage. His mother was getting out and the captain was opening the gate for her. And as Ronnie dawdled by a bush he heard him say, 'Adios,' and saw him wink at her – *wink!* – before he jumped into the jeep and drove off.

And there, in the front garden, just straightening up from his gooseberries, was Uncle Will, who must have seen that wink, judging by the scowl on his face.

'Getting reg'lar, this transport stuff. On the long way round to Braintree again, is he?'

Ronnie's mum seemed a bit flustered. 'It's where he lives, He's renting a cottage. Somewhere on the edge.'

"Spect he c'n afford it, on his dollars. You didn't see the boy on the road, then?' The old man had spotted Ronnie, who was trying to go round the back quietly. 'Must've drove right past him.'

This was impossible, Ronnie knew, because he'd come from Evie's direction.

And now the lying began; because while Ronnie needed to keep his secret about going to Evie's, he wanted to give his mum some hope about his dad; a bit of news that would make her think about him being alive – of having someone in her head other than the American captain. As soon as they were alone in the kitchen, he told her about Evie's father, how she and her mum had been shown a picture of him for identification.

'She told me at school today. They'd given him

up, see. Thought they weren't ever going to see him again, not getting any letters or anything.'

'How could she tell you at school, if she was in London all day?' His mother had seen through him. He'd been right to worry; he definitely wasn't a born liar. 'We tell the truth and shame the devil, you and me, Ron. I'm not having you keeping your friend secret because of that stupid old man's prejudice about Italians.'

But, thinking about it, Ronnie didn't want them turfed out of Greengates and having to find another cottage to share. Which was all mixed up with him wanting his mum to feel hopeful about his dad – even while she was driving around in the American captain's jeep. 'It could be the same with Dad. It could be that some time we'll get good news like that, right out of nowhere...'

His mother smiled at him, but right now her eyes were a black pool again. 'Don't get your hopes up too high, Ron. Think the worst, and you're never going to be disappointed.'

This, Ronnie realised, was just what he was starting to do: thinking – or fearing – the worst. But not so much about his dad right now as about her.

Chapter Five

Evie didn't show up at school all that week – which left him flat and low again. The feeling of his arm round her shoulder, her cheek against his, had been something special. And because Uncle Will wanted Ronnie to help out at the cottage, he didn't have a chance to find himself accidentally at the railway carriage. The old man set him to work picking apples at the top of the garden. And Ronnie was up in the branches of a Granny Smith that Friday evening when he heard the boring voice of Uncle Len beneath him.

'Good to see you being useful.' This was very different from the fight with windfalls Ronnie would have had with his dad. And Uncle Len being there meant they were in for a long, boring weekend – smoked like kippers by Uncle Will's roll-ups and Uncle Len's pipe.

But that was nothing compared with the choke on the Saturday, when the American captain brought Ronnie's mum home in the jeep again – but not from work, and not at half past six – but at twelve o'clock at night.

Ronnie had gone to bed. His mother had told him she was going to a dance at the base with the other girls, so he'd taken his paraffin lamp upstairs at bedtime. But he didn't sleep – and, anyway, the whole village must have been woken by the sound of the jeep bringing his mother home. And by the time he'd turned up the lamp and got down the stairs Uncle Len and Uncle Will were already out of the living-room and in the hallway.

'Oh, you're safe, then, Ivy.'

'We've been worried about you.'

'Them Yanks ain't no gentlemen...'

Ronnie's mother stared at them. Ronnie knew that look, and it meant trouble.

'The Americans I know are all perfect gentlemen, thank you. And Clay Miller is a married man...'

'Don't mean nothing, miles away from home...'

And the argument turned into tears. Ronnie's mum cried, and Ronnie went to her. But, 'Back to bed!' she said, harshly. So he went. The voices went quiet, the uncles muttering in the living-room and his mother in the kitchen washing her face. But the worst thing she said was when she came up.

'We don't have to live here, Len, so don't think we do. This isn't our only option down here.'

And as the draughty spectres from the lamp danced across the bedroom walls, Ronnie knew what that option was; and it really kept him awake.

He lay there in silence until morning.

✗✗✗

Getting up to go to school on Monday, Ronnie had made his decision. Whether he did it in a nasty way or a nice way, he knew what he had to do about Evie. Imagining his arm round her shoulder, cheek-to-cheek, Jane Russell eyes, long brown legs, the thought of her hurt him – but there was no way that he could be her friend. He couldn't be her school friend, and he couldn't be her home friend. He couldn't be her boyfriend and she couldn't be his girlfriend. He wasn't going to make Uncle Will's hatred of Italians send him and his mother to where he knew she'd go if they were turfed out: to the American captain's cottage in Braintree.

But it wasn't easy. Not being friendly didn't come naturally to Ronnie. At school that Monday morning, his heart sank at the sight of Evie there in the playground – and in a Jane Russell cowgirl shirt. He turned off in the other direction, to start teaching buzz-ball to the younger boys. At first Evie took no notice; but when it was time to carry in the full milk crate from the shade of the school wall, she confronted him.

'We do the milk bottles together,' she said, leaning against the wall with her bare arm barring him from getting to the porch.

'Not last week, we didn't.' Ronnie couldn't believe he was saying this.

'It's my birthday, Wednesday. My mum's took to you, said you could come to tea.' But she was frowning; Ronnie could see how unsure of things this bold-as-brass girl could be.

'I've got to go somewhere, Wednesday. Sorry.'

'We could have it Thursday...'

It hurt, imagining a birthday tea, and a birthday kiss. People kissed on birthdays. It was expected.

Ronnie took the weight of the crate on his thigh. 'I'm doing something Thursday, too.'

She stood up straight. 'What's up with you, Warren?' Not Ron, or even Ronnie, but Warren. 'You sound just like some of the others'

'Don't know what you're talking about!'

'Have they got at you? Think I'm *different*, do you?'

'No!'

'Think I'm an Eyetie enemy?'

'No!' God, he didn't. Looking at her beautiful, puzzled face, he knew just what he thought of her – this girl he never stopped thinking about. 'Look out, this crate's heavy,' he said, hoisting it up again.

And she moved aside, well aside, as he carried the crate of milk bottles into the infants' classroom.

✕✕✕

It was a hell of a rotten week; and Ronnie's life looked like being rotten for ever. Uncle Will was a misery and Uncle Len was a pain. People were talking about how the Germans were sending over massive rockets that whooshed down out of space and demolished whole streets in London. His dad was 'missing', probably out east, judging by the letters they'd had, and according to people in the Three Ashes there were horrible things going on in the Japanese prisoner-of-war camps. And what was his mum up to with the American captain?

On top of all that, the only lift in his life – Evie Michaels – was what the Americans called 'off limits'. All day long she was there, and all day long he had to pretend he wished she wasn't; and now she was behaving exactly like him. She filled the inkwells and left him to carry the milk. They only shared what they had to – hymn books and poetry books, and when they did, she held her hand as far away as possible from his.

What was worse, Evie thought Ronnie was against her for being Italian, when he wasn't. In fact, sometimes his stomach rolled with dread when Uncle Will started to go on about Eyeties – because Ronnie knew this would infuriate his mother, and she'd up and off to Braintree – and then he'd have given up Evie for no reason.

Like the bushes at the top of the garden, everything had become so tangled. Up there among the scratches, instead of becoming soft and sweet, the blackberries had turned out to be hard and sour –

just as Evie Michaels seemed to be this week.

Frustration churned in Ronnie like a bilious attack.

And then, when he thought he couldn't feel any lower – Ronnie's mother came home from work in the jeep on the Thursday with more sour fruit for Ronnie.

'You don't mind if I'm out for a couple of hours, Saturday afternoon, do you?' They were in the kitchen, getting the tea. 'Two of the squadrons are going over to France to fly from there – they're saying goodbye with a barbecue.'

Ronnie's hopes suddenly rose. 'What's-his-name – is he going to France?'

'Captain Miller? No, thank goodness. They need him here.'

Well, I don't! thought Ronnie. Because his mum would be gallivanting around with the American airman, all pretty and done up in her best dress.

Ronnie muttered about having to do something – he didn't know what – and went off to the top of the garden, to stare at the green blackberries in their tangle, trying to puzzle out what to do about all this. And as he stood there, he thought of the ravine at the edge of the common where the Plumstead blackberries grew – until he and the lads picked them. And how did they do that? They had a stick and wore a glove to get a firm grip on the thorny branches. When you're using a glove and a stick, you can pull the berries to you, make them bend your way.

Ronnie suddenly realised that he had an answer to his problem. He'd bend things himself, take things into his own hands. It would be hard, and he'd have to be bold. But he was Reg Warren's son, wasn't he? Reg Warren would have done it – and so would he.

Chapter Six

Ronnie didn't have a watch, so he had to go by the clock on Uncle Will's mantelpiece. Half-past six was about the time his mother came home in the jeep. The American captain always got out and opened the gate for her, then saluted, or winked, or patted her arm, and watched her go round the back before he drove off. So if Ronnie was ready by a quarter-past six he should be about right. Uncle Will's gooseberry bushes made a good hiding-place in the corner of the front garden; and that's where Ronnie would be crouching. Then he'd do what had to be done.

Friday at school was miserable again, made worse by thoughts of what he was going to do that evening. They sent icy tremors down his back, and his face felt as if it was wearing a tight mask. When the teacher said 'Chairs up!' and 'Dismiss!' he got himself home as quickly as he could to do some more thinking out in the privy and up in the bedroom; but he knew somehow he had to avoid being given a job by Uncle Will. Nothing was going to stop him carrying out his plan. He stayed in his long trousers – tonight he was going to be a man.

And at last it was time. When the cottage was empty and Uncle Will was out at the back among his cabbages, a few minutes after six o'clock Ronnie went out to the front and hunched down tight into his gooseberry bush hiding-place. He waited. And he waited. Flies found him interesting. Ants looked for a new home up his trousers. Bees menaced him like fighters round an enemy bomber. But at last he heard it – the sound of the American Army Air Force jeep coming along The Street. He tensed himself, and nearly poked his eye out on a branch trying to see over the fence.

The jeep pulled up, and out got the captain, smart as ever in his shirt-sleeve-order uniform. He strode round to the offside to open the gate for Ronnie's mum.

'There you go, ma'am. Till tomorrow, Ivy.'

Now for it! Ronnie had a ten-second chance.

As the American captain stood at the gate and his mother slipped through it like a girl doing country dancing, he made his move. The jeep had its canvas top pulled up against the sun and the struts got in his way, but without a door to slow him down, he was up and over the sill in seconds, sliding behind the driver's seat and crouching in the back even before he heard the closing click of the gate. Keeping as low as he could, he just had to hope that the captain wouldn't check anything behind him before driving off.

He didn't, thank goodness. The airman slung his cap on the dashboard and drove fast along the rutted roads, throwing Ronnie about as he whistled a tune Ronnie didn't know. The jeep was pretty basic – the front seats seemed to have normal leg-room, but in the back Ronnie was kneeling sideways on and in pain.

But somehow he stuck it. Every time they stopped – at crossroads or traffic lights – he thought they had reached the Braintree cottage, and his insides rolled, thinking how he was going to stand up to that dirty dog Clay Miller and tell him to leave his mum alone. The man had no business to be treating her special. She'd been injured in the Blitz. She was upset about moving out of her own house. She was worried about Ronnie's dad being missing. What with Uncle Will and Uncle Len and life in their behind-the-times cottage, she just wasn't herself any more. And it was wartime, when people did things they wouldn't dream of doing in peacetime...

Several more stops, and then the jeep pulled up with a jerk and the ignition was turned off. They must be at the American captain's place. So this was it! Ronnie's stomach rolled worse than before. His throat had gone dry. He looked up at the corrugated iron cottage – more a small shack – and watched the American captain jump out. He didn't want to be caught crouching there in the back of the jeep. He wanted to stand to his full height and look all of his fourteen-and-a-half years.

Right, Captain Carl Miller – watch out!

The American captain was on the pavement straightening his uniform. Suddenly he seemed bigger and tougher. But there was no going back. Ronnie was going to tell him where to get off, face to face. He was going to put the tin lid on any more of that silly stuff with his mum.

He climbed out of the jeep and came to the front of the jeep, his legs shaking.

The captain heard him, turned. 'Hey! What

the deuce is this?' He frowned at Ronnie.

'I've come to…' But the words in Ronnie's head had gone for a burton. How do you tell a man to leave your mother alone? Or do you just run at him and punch him in the belly?

'You're a long way off base, son…'

Or head-butt him?

'Hi, Airman!' a voice called.

The captain looked away towards the cottage, where a woman was standing in its doorway, pretty, younger than Ronnie's mum, leaning against the woodwork with an arm up – as if to say, 'Come on in, cowboy,' the way Jane Russell did in *The Outlaw*.

'Honey…' The captain ran to her, picked her up by the waist and twirled her around.

'Hello, Clay.' She sounded English. She let the captain hold her in the air until he'd kissed her – a proper kiss.

'Who've you got there?' she asked.

The captain turned back. 'It's Ronnie Warren.' he said. 'Ivy's boy.' He looked a bit puzzled.

Now, what should Ronnie say? This was a shock-and-a-half. He thought he'd find an empty cottage with a spare bedroom for him and his mum. Instead, here was this woman holding on to the captain's arm all lovey-dovey as they came over to him. And this titchy shack hardly had room for the two of them…

'Why, the little critter,' said the captain. 'He's stowed away for a joy ride!'

Ronnie picked up on this. 'Yeah. Sort of stowed away. I'm sorry, I tried the seat in the back – but before I could get out you drove off fast.'

'He's a right fast one, is Clay,' the woman said. 'Speedy's his middle name.' And they looked at one another and laughed.

'This is Ronnie Warren,' said the captain, and Ronnie shook hands with the woman. 'Ivy showed you his picture at the Saturday dance. Ronnie, this is my wife, Vera Miller.'

His wife?

'Howdy,' Ronnie said.

'So you're Ronnie. Just as good-looking as your snap. We had a good old chat, your mum and me – between working our arms off serving those thirsty airmen. Pleased to meet you.'

Ronnie's face had gone stiff as he kept a fixed smile on it. *So his mum hadn't been dancing and gallivanting with the American captain – she'd been working hard behind the bar with the captain's wife! Now he didn't know what to say again – so he just* stood there, feeling devastated that he'd got everything wrong. Captain Clay Miller didn't live on his own. He had a pretty wife. And he didn't have spare space in this cottage for more than a cat.

The man wasn't an enemy – he was a friend. An ally.

'Do you want to come to the barbecue tomorrow?' Vera Miller was asking. 'I'm going myself – helping your mum again, behind the bar...'

'Yeah...' Ronnie said. 'Like to.'

He must still have had a puzzled look on his face, because Vera explained, 'I'm a GI bride. A Braintree girl who fell for a hunky Yank...'

'We've been fixing on having you and your ma over to tea for some time,' Clay Miller said.

'That'd be nice,' Ronnie found himself saying.

'So, it's a soda and then I'll run you home. But I tell you, I'm real glad you didn't tap me on the shoulder while I was driving. There's plenty enough aircrew ghosts around the base to give us all the heebie-jeebies...'

'Thanks very much,' said Ronnie; and he went into the cool of the cottage for his 'soda' – which was American for lemonade – and as he sat in a deckchair in the small plot at the back, he found that his mind was already made up about what he was going to do next.

If he and his mother got turfed out of Greengates for any reason, then they'd find a place like this to rent, or they'd take their chances back in London. Now that this American captain's cottage business was settled, he could talk to her about it. They didn't have to live under the thumbs of those two uncles – which meant he was going to have whatever friend he wanted, English or Italian. So when Clay Miller drove him back to Chalkney Green, he would ask him not to drop him off at home, but at Evie's place. He'd got a lot of explaining to do and grovelling apologies to make. And if she didn't want to listen the first time, he'd keep on and on until she did. He had a very important peace to make. And peace was one of the dearest things he wanted in all the world.

And fizz. Peace and fizz.

Man of the House

Chapter One

'You're being so pig-headed, Ronnie – you're throwing your future away!'

'*Ronnie*', not '*Ron*'. That meant she was being the boss.

'No, I'm not. I'm on a good rate. They've moved me up off the bottom already, after two days…'

As usual, the dispute was in the kitchen, standing eating their toast and trying to drink their tea too hot. Ronnie was on the six-to-two shift at Johnson and Philips cable works, and his mother started at seven-thirty, up at the Optical Buildings – another early morning breakfast taken at a run.

'And where will it lead? Nowhere. Dead end.' She had her back to Ronnie, at the grill – which was why this sort of talk always happened in the kitchen:

it was less eyeball-to-eyeball.

'Spot-welding's semi-skilled – and it could lead anywhere…'

'Listen.' She turned round to face him, waving a burnt piece of toast. 'Open the back door.'

Ronnie opened it. She threw out the toast and stood in the doorwary. 'The Germans have stopped fighting. We've got peace in Europe. So what's going to happen? There'll be a shortage of jobs with everyone coming back from the war…'

'Not everyone.'

'That's by the way.'

But it had hit home. She looked away and took in a deep breath, and Ronnie regretted having said it. There had been no word about his dad for nearly four years, and they both knew that by now he had to be dead. This was why Ronnie was being pig-headed, as she called it.

'If you'd gone to Matchless Engineering, they were going to consider you for an apprenticeship in September. A trade. Letters after your name…'

'Yes. P–O–O–R. Two or three days in college, and rotten wages for five years.'

'Short-sighted, that is. Your dad served his time…'

Ronnie threw his own uneaten toast into the bin and ran his plate under the cold tap. 'But Dad's not here – and I am. I'm the man of the house now, Mum, and I'm not having you going out to work till I'm nearly twenty.'

Besides which, he could save up for a Silver Hawk motor-bike a lot quicker at Johnson and Philips than he would at Matchless. He'd worked it all out. He could take his mum out on the pillion, down to Margate, over to Southend, show her a bit of the life she was missing; and in under the hour he could get across to Essex to see Evie Michaels.

His mother finished wafting out the toast smoke and slammed the back door. 'It's early May, Ronnie, and the interview's in June. You've got to get that reply in.'

'I've got to get some decent money in this household, off my own bat – that's what I've got to do.' And he went through to the hall to grab his bike and cycle over to Johnson and Philips at Charlton.

'You forgot your dinner.' His mother followed him with his wrapped-up sandwiches and flask.

He stuffed them into his saddlebag. 'Ta.' He kissed her. Ever since he'd been ten and the bomb had dropped on Auntie Edna's, he'd made sure they never went their own ways on harsh words. 'See you tonight.'

'Yeah… See you tonight.'

He scooted a few yards on a pedal as she quickly shut the front door. And Ronnie knew why. She never liked him to see her cry.

✗✗✗

'Oi! Ronnie. I want you a minute…'

Ronnie was in the welding shop of the cable makers. As a new boy, he was being told about the next job coming into the shop: casings for industrial water heaters.

'What Winston Churchill wanted used to come first, but now we're looking to civvy street again,' the shop foreman was telling him. But Stan Cardiff from the next shop had just put his head round the door.

'Can I borrow your boy, Bert?' he asked.

'What d'you want him for?' Ronnie's foreman asked.

'Only a quick errand. Can you spare him? My lad's on his break.'

Bert Powell looked from one to the other – the lathe operator from the milling shop and this new boy. He smiled. 'Yeah, all right, if it's quick. I've only got 'im till two.'

Ronnie went over to the doorway. 'Yes?'

'I want you to…' Stan Cardiff put the back of his hand over his mouth, and coughed. 'I want you to go up the stores an' get me a tin of grease…'

'A tin of grease…' Ronnie repeated.

'A special sort. Tell Dennis: the milling shop's running out so we want some elbow grease.'

'Some elbow gr—' Ronnie stopped. He could see Stan trying to keep a straight face. 'Oh yeah?' he said, 'Like the paint shop foreman sent me for a tin of gloss yesterday – sky-blue-pink.'

The two old hands cracked out their laughs. 'You won't catch this one, not no more,' Bert said. ' 'E's got 'is 'ead screwed on the right way.'

Ronnie went back to solving the puzzle of assembling water heater panels. He could take a good joke – but by his third day, looking a daisy in front of the stores manager was wearing a bit thin.

Stan Cardiff hadn't finished, though. 'I'll tell you something else,' he said, turning serious. 'They reckon we're all having the day off tomorrow. Including you welding boys, Bert…'

'Yeah, thanks. We'll go down Margate, shall we,

son? Jolly-boys' outing. Roll our trousers up an' 'ave a paddle...?'

But Ronnie certainly knew what he'd do with a day off. He'd make an early start, get the workmen's train up to London, and go down to Chalkley Green to see Evie. He knew the way well by now. And if he ever had a day off next year when he'd passed sixteen, he'd go there on a second-hand Silver Hawk, to take her out for a spin.

'I'm not having you on. It's in the *Daily Mirror*. They reckon we've all got the day off tomorrow. It's coming on the wireless tonight. Tomorrow's going to be Victory Day. Official. Public holiday.'

'Wow!'

'Good ol' Winston Churchill!'

The men and the boys in the welding shop clattered their tools.

'Yeah – Victory in Europe Day! So the guv'nor says we've got to work double hard today to make up production time.'

'Right, that's it, then, lads,' Bert told the shop, 'let's buckle down to it.'

But Ronnie found it difficult to concentrate on water heater casings. Yes, he thought, everyone said the war was over – in Europe. But there was still a hell of a lot of fighting going on in the Far East…

'Cheer up, son, it's good news. A day off, an' it ain't Sunday or Bank 'oliday.'

'I know…'

Bert Powell ran a hand along the heater panel he was showing Ronnie, deliberately not looking at him. 'Everyone's alive till you're told they're dead, like my old dad in the last war. Come 'ome from a civvy 'ospital in Constantinople. Not a word from no one. An' you know what they say about the Red Cross…'

'What?'

'Well, you take the war out east where you reckon your dad might've been. They say the Red Cross can't get into them Japanese prisoner-of-war camps. That lot don' go along with the rules of war…'

If this was meant to cheer up Ronnie, it didn't work. What he'd heard about the vicious war in the Far East didn't give him hope, it killed it.

✗✗✗

It was like a new country laid out before him, stretching so far into the distance that his eyes ached, just looking at how far it went. But instead of trees or hills to stare at, it was lights on both sides of the river, all twinkling white: miles and miles of streetlamps, switched on for the first time in five years. They were distant memories for Ronnie.

After a quick tea, he and his mother had come up to the highest part of Plumstead to see them. And tomorrow, Tuesday 8th May, was going to be celebration time. On their way up the hill they had passed people putting up flags and bunting or repainting the victory signs on their walls, and one sign had suddenly saddened them: a banner across the street which said, 'WELCOME HOME ALF – WAR HERO'. Every day men were coming back from the war: soldiers, sailors, airmen and women – and prisoners-of-war released from their camps in Germany. But that wouldn't be the case with Reg Warren. No new telegram had come, no letter, no airgraph. The celebration next day would mostly be for other people.

And right now, Ronnie knew his dad was on his mother's mind because, as she talked about these evening lights, her voice had gone flat. 'Before the war we could see them going on, borough by borough, on the other side of the river.' Her eyes were over there, with her words.

'Did you and Dad use to come up here?'

She gave a small laugh. '"Walking out", they called it. Courting. And your dad always said this was the best sunset view in London, next after me.' She pointed to the west. 'There's St Paul's.' She cleared her throat:

'Earth hath not anything to show more fair... I don't know all the words.

Ships, towers, domes, theatres, and temples lie

Open to the fields, and to the sky... But your dad knew it off by heart...'

Her voice had run out of the courage to continue.

Ronnie put his arm around her waist.

'He had a good mind, your dad, which he put to good use.'

While Ronnie was wasting his for better money in the short run – that was her message. But he didn't loosen his grip.

'*So!*' Her voice changed so suddenly, it made Ronnie jump. 'Are we going up to London to celebrate tomorrow? To lift our chins up proudly at the King and Queen and old Winnie? For you and me? And for my Edna? And for your dad?'

'Yes,' Ronnie answered quickly. 'We'll do that.' He wouldn't go over to Chalkley Green. He'd put that off until the weekend.

'We'll get a 53A to Horse Guards Parade and walk down the Mall to Buckingham Palace.'

'No.' Ronnie surprised her. 'We won't do that.'

She frowned at him.

'We'll get a 53A to Horse Guards and *march* down the Mall to Buckingham Palace – like Royal Artillery soldiers…'

'That's it, Ron; that's what we'll do,' she agreed. Like… Royal… Artillery… soldiers…'

Chapter Two

Having VE Day off was a treat, like a school half-term holiday – something that Ronnie didn't get any more.

His mother had the day off, too. Back at the Optical Buildings she was grinding lenses for the RAF boys in the Far East, but, war work or not, VE Day was a holiday. So neither of them had to go to work, and as it wasn't the weekend, there was a strange feeling of 'what shall we do?' until the time came to go up to London and march down the Mall. They didn't want to decorate the house with flags and bunting because there was only one decoration they'd ever want to tie across the front of the house – and that was a hero's banner. So, while his mother gave the gas stove what she called 'a birthday', Ronnie went out for a mooch: hands in pockets, down to the common for a game of cricket. But he couldn't be sure there would be one. Now that he was out at work, there wasn't a gang of boys to make arrangements with any more.

All over the houses on the way to the common, Union Jacks flew and bunting fluttered, and in one of the gardens a washing line of red, white, and blue knickers gave Ronnie's feet a lively jaunt as he walked past. The war was over. He wouldn't be bombed again. And he could live in his own house for as long as he liked. Things were back to the way they were in peacetime – except for not having a dad any more. But there was something he would never admit to anyone: he could no longer hear the sound of his dad's voice in his head any more. There were photographs at home, so he could see his dad; but he couldn't hear him these days. That part of him was gone – the start of a life-long loss...

Nothing was happening on the common – except for a boy Ronnie knew who was throwing sticks for his dog, Terry Boulter, still long and lanky, and probably still a rotten footballer.

"Ello! Wotcha, Ronnie.'

'Wotcha, Tez. What're you doing?'

'Throwing sticks for me dog.'

'No, what are you doing, like, for work – or did you pass for grammar school?'

'Post Office. G.P.O.'

'Ah.'

'What about you?'

'Johnson and Phillips. An' saving up for a motorbike.'

'Useful, that. I only crank me pushbike.'

'I've got my eye on a Silver Hawk one day.'

Now the dog was barking for the stick to be thrown, so Terry said cheerio and loped off across the common. Ronnie sat on the grass and thought about Evie, the girl his Silver Hawk would take him to, when he got one.

She had forgiven him for his unfriendliness back at Chalkney Green school – not at first, but she came round in the end, when she'd calmed down enough for him to share his secret fears. 'Like a ruddy film, you are,' she said. And by the time his mother decided they were coming back to London, he and Evie were sort-of 'walking out' – which Ronnie thought weren't quite the right words for being up apple trees and bending along lines of late potatoes. But what a smashing girlfriend to have, thought Ronnie –

someone who fizzed you whatever you were doing!

✕✕✕

At three o'clock they listened to Winnie – Winston Churchill – on the wireless. They sat there concentrating, the way they always did for the news on the Home Service.

> *'We may allow ourselves a brief period of rejoicing; but let us not forget for a moment the toil and efforts that lie ahead. Japan, with all her treachery and greed, remains unsubdued.'*

Ronnie stole a quick look at his mother. Her lips were pursed, as if it was her mouth rather than her eyes that was holding back tears.

> *'The injury she has inflicted on Great Britain, the United States, and other countries, and her detestable cruelties, call for justice and retribution.'*

Another quick look, and she was nodding at the wireless as if the set was Winston Churchill himself. They both knew that the Royal Artillery had gone to the Far East, something he and she didn't talk about any more.

We must now devote all our strength and resources to the completion of our task, both at home and abroad. Advance, Britannia! Long live the cause of freedom! God save the King!'

Ronnie's mother suddenly got up and went to the door. 'I'm getting out a good frock,' she said, her voice choking in her throat. She went upstairs. And Ronnie suddenly wondered what she was keeping from him. What had she heard? What was she going to tell him when she thought the time was right, after the war was properly over? *Had a telegram come one day when she was in and he was out?*

So he left the upstairs to her. He'd look out his Victory Day shirt a bit later on.

✗✗✗

There wasn't to be any marching down the Mall like the Royal Artillery. From Trafalgar Square all the way along to Buckingham Palace it was more like sailing on a choppy tide, people weaving and waving, sudden jigging forwards one moment, sideways the next. With everyone in the highest spirits, even an elbow in the cheek wasn't complained about – it was part of the jubilation. Arms were linked, then dropped. Everyone was in step one moment – the next, they were tripping over one another, now in front, now behind, over there, then back here. Ronnie recognised the different uniforms: the ATS girls, the WAAFs, the WRNS, all being flirty, while the serving men had faces covered in kisses. There were Americans, Canadians, Poles, French, Australians, and British lads in their Number Ones – Tommies from different regiments, the 'Brylcreem boys' of the RAF, and the sailors who couldn't stop having their uniform 'dickies' touched for luck. Plus the Land Army girls, and firemen and nurses from the home front – while an ARP warden collected coins in his steel helmet for a street party in Bermondsey.

And a sudden thought hit Ronnie as he saw a pretty girl giving an American airman a kiss: what if Evie was here somewhere? People had come from all over the country. London was as tight-packed as a Charlton-Arsenal match, and Evie had always been up for whatever was going on. These days she was working in Woolworths in Braintree. Well, what if those shop girls had all come up for VE Day? His eyes tried to take in everyone, here in the road and up there too – because people were climbing on anything they could – trees, statues, lamp posts, with others paddling in the fountains under Nelson's Column. One girl took his eye, lifting up her skirt and doing a dance in the water for the benefit of a newsreel camera. She wasn't Evie, though – and thank goodness for that!

Ronnie's mother jumped, as a firework was let off nearby. 'We had enough of that in the Blitz!' she complained; but she didn't let it spoil anything. Streamers were thrown, flags waved, and rude songs sung about Hitler, with the weather hot and the air rising above London to shimmer in a noisy haze of happiness. But all the time over Ronnie's face lay the chill knowledge that his dad wasn't here sharing the celebration.

It didn't take much to raise his spirits, though, as he and his mother were pushed and pulled in the crush outside Buckingham Palace. Suddenly, Ronnie caught sight of some famous people he was seeing for the first time in the flesh – not in the newspapers or the cinema newsreels, but up there in real life, on the balcony of the Palace: King George and Queen Elizabeth, and Princess Elizabeth in her ATS uniform. They waved as the throats of the crowd grew hoarse calling back to them. And... and... there he was! People jumped. People pointed. Everyone waved and cheered. All at once Ronnie's heart was pumped up to bursting, when he saw the man they were all shouting at, coming out to stand next to the king. It was the Prime Minister and war leader, the man Ronnie had heard on the wireless only a few hours before: Winston Churchill – bowing deep and low to the crowd.

Ronnie looked at his mother, crushed there beside him. She was cheering while her eyes streamed with tears – the most gut-wrenching sight he'd ever seen in his life.

Which was when a sailor put his hat on her head at a jaunty angle, the gold lettering of 'HMS' on the ribbon glinting in the lights. 'What a port to come home to!' the sailor said, and kissed her on the cheek. And he turned her face towards the newsreel camera that had fought its own way through the crowd. 'What beauties we've got in Blighty!' he shouted into the camera lens – before whisking his hat off Ivy's head and disappearing in the crowd.

'Well!' Ronnie's mother said. 'Anything goes

today, I suppose!' And in the mad elation of the moment she shoved Ronnie forward to join the end of a line of people dancing the conga around the Victoria Memorial, leading off back down the Mall. One-two-three-kick, one-two-three-kick! With his arms thrust forward Ronnie found himself holding tight to a girl's silky waist.

'I came, I saw, I conga'd!
I came I saw I conga'd!
Aye, aye conga!
Aye, aye, conga!'

The girl in front should have been Evie Michaels; and then he'd have held on for ever. As it was, his mother got out of breath halfway back to Trafalgar Square and they took themselves away. But while others went to find a drink in a pub or a quiet place in St James's Park for a cuddle with a new friend, as dusk fell and searchlights made the shape of a 'V for Victory' in the sky, Ronnie and his mother took a last look down the Mall.

'Home.'

With a quick nod at one another, they headed for the 53A bus stop, and Flaxton Road, Plumstead,

with Ronnie's feelings in a mix – because he'd helped
to celebrate the victory in Europe, which people like
his dad would never be able to enjoy.

Chapter Three

'What am I going to say to people if it's shown at the pictures?'

'If what's shown at the pictures?' Ronnie was looking at the *Daily Mail*. He was going to cut out and keep the pictures of the King and Queen and Winston Churchill on the balcony.

His mother looked over his shoulder and tut-tutted at a picture of a girl with a sailor's hat on her head. But it wasn't her. This girl was standing in a fountain in Trafalgar Square.

'He was up so close, that newsreel man!'

'What newsreel man? What are you talking about, Mum?'

'You know…'

'No, I don't.'

'Well, what would people say? We've lost your dad – and there I am outside the palace with 'HMS' on my head and being kissed by a sailor...'

Ronnie looked up at her and winked. 'They'd say you were a jolly good sport!'

'Huh! Ron, I want to know if they're going to show that on a newsreel. I need to get to the cinema.' She'd brought in the toast, but she was holding it absent-mindedly, her mind far away. 'I tell you, I'd like to know, before your Uncle Len gets to see it down in Southend.'

They were having a late breakfast up at the table. The next day had been made into a public holiday, too, so that people could hold street parties for the children. And, of course, to go to the pictures to see the celebrations and embarrassments of the day before.

'You'll come with me, won't you, Ron? You'll help me get home in one piece if I see my face up on that screen...?'

'What are you gonna do – faint?'

'I don't know what I'd do, with the shame of it...'

Ronnie laughed. 'We'll listen for the doorbell. It might be the film people wanting a replacement for Jane Russell.'

'Don't be funny! I've just got to know…'

'So, what's on at the pictures?' If Ronnie was going to miss a chance to get over to Essex, it might as well be for a good film. Otherwise, it wasn't worth their one-and-threepences just to see five minutes of newsreel between the main pictures.

His mother eventually put down the toast and sat leaning her elbows on the table. 'What did it say on his hat?' she asked.

'"HMS." They don't say "HMS Whatever", in case of Japanese spies. That would let them know which ships were back here.'

'No!' Ronnie's mother grabbed a piece of toast and margarined it so hard that it broke into fragments. 'The newsreel man's hat? He had a ticket on it, like the Mad Hatter.'

Now Ronnie knew what she was going on about. The Odeon at Woolwich showed one newsreel, and the Granada a different one. One newsreel had a cockerel crowing at the start and the other had searchlights, but he couldn't remember which was which. He shut his eyes and tried to picture the cameraman's hat in his head – but the day before had turned into a red, white and blue blur.

'We'll go to one cinema tonight, and the other on Saturday.' She stared across the table at Ronnie.

'Twice in one week? We definitely need my wages.'

She ignored that. 'I need to know, Ron. I just need to know.'

Ronnie flapped the *Daily Mail* noisily, the way his father sometimes had, like a newspaper coughing. 'Not forgetting the Century in Beresford Square, and the Bexleyheath Palace,' he said. 'That'll take care of Monday and Tuesday nights, too.' And he ducked, as she threw her toast at him.

'You don't get it! You don't get it, do you?' she shouted. 'I want your dad remembered decently along this street; not the dead husband of a stupid wife being kissed by a sailor in full view of royalty.'

There was nothing to say in reply to this, so Ronnie kept quiet – and kissed goodbye to his chance of going over to see Evie Michaels.

xxx

Suddenly Ivy Warren remembered. The cameraman's hat had said 'Pathé News', which would mean the Granada, she reckoned. She was pretty sure it was the

Granada and not the Odeon that showed the news with a cockerel crowing. And the film showing was *Son of Lassie* – which was a double disappointment to Ronnie; because not only would he have to sit through that soppy cinema organist they had at the Granada, but another Lassie film as well. Even as a young kid, he hadn't liked the first one. Now, Jane Russell in *The Outlaw* – a new one of those would have been all right.

On the other hand, he told himself, doing something for his mum would be good. VE Day had brought that sad look into her eyes again. She would be missing his dad more than ever this week, with all the banners flying for soldiers coming home, and all those soldiers, sailors, and airmen back in London. He missed his dad too – but nowadays he had Evie to think about, and what with saving up to get a Silver Hawk, he had his life in front of him. For his mother, though, everything was in the past. Getting excited about things lay behind her. So going to the pictures tonight would definitely be the right thing to do.

✗✗✗

They were going to be late. There was no fixed start time – the films rolled on continuously from about one o'clock in the afternoon. You queued up and you went in when there were vacant seats, usually in the middle of a picture, and you came out three hours later when you came round to the place in the film where you went in. There were always two films showing, the main picture and a not-so-good one called the B film, with trailers and adverts in between, and at the Granada an organ played, followed by the newsreel. Even so, they were going to miss the last showing of the newsreel if they didn't get down to Woolwich by eight o'clock. And they were late – because Ronnie's mother had decided to help out at the kids' victory party along Barden Street.

People had been collecting money for this, and today they'd set out two long tables in a V shape, covered with clean, white sheets since no one possessed table-cloths that long. Everyone had been saving their ration book coupons to buy extra sweets and jellies; and Martin's, the corner shop, had given free lemonade, providing the empties were returned. And when the organisers had knocked on Ivy Warren's door for contributions, she'd donated a sheet, and had suddenly decided to put on a paper hat and a clean pinafore, and had gone to help serve the children. Ronnie – feeling far too grown-up to sit down with the kids – had hovered on the pavement, and helped with chairs and one or two of the games. Now they were going to have to run to the bus stop if they were going to see that newsreel.

Ronnie's mother had wanted 'a nice wash' and a clean frock for going to the pictures. 'You don't know who might be there,' she said, 'and even if I look a sight on the screen, I want to look decent in real life.'

'Do you really think you'll be in it?' Ronnie wanted to know. 'With all those people he was filming?'

'I really don't know, Ron,' his mother answered tartly. 'But to my mind he did seem to linger.'

'Well, we won't know, if you don't get a move on.'

'Thank you, Ron. Yes, I know. Have we got some coppers for the bus?' She was upstairs by now, calling down.

Ronnie jingled some coins. 'Yeah. If they haven't put all the 53As on the scrapheap by the time we get to the bus stop...'

'Ha-ha, funny boy!' She came down the stairs.

She looked a treat. She was wearing a frock he hadn't seen before. She must have been saving her clothing coupons for it. It was in a red, white and blue polka-dot pattern with a shortish skirt. And from the look of her legs, she was wearing a new pair of silk stockings, with high-heeled shoes. Her hair was done up in rolled waves – no wonder she'd taken so long over it – and at the side of her head was a Royal Artillery hairclip, specially made for the wives and sweethearts of soldiers – and their widows.

She looked at Ronnie, daring him to say anything.

So he did. 'You look a peach,' he told her. 'A real peach.'

'Do I?' She checked her lipstick in the hall mirror and turned to him. 'I wanted to wear this yesterday, but I didn't dare. It'll be all right in the pictures, in the dark…'

This seemed a daft thing to say, after all the trouble she'd taken.

'I'd want your dad to be as proud of me as I am of him.' She kept her voice straight. And Ronnie knew his mum thought that his dad would be looking down from heaven, and seeing her like he'd used to, in the sunset.

But the lump in Ronnie's throat came from picturing his dad lying, all blood and bones, at the feet of a grinning Japanese soldier.

'Come on, then,' she said. 'Get your skates on or we'll be late.'

And he couldn't find the voice to ask her whose fault that would be...

Chapter Four

Ronnie was just about to open the front door when a shadow appeared in the crinkled glass.

'Mrs Johnson,' he hissed. 'Tell her we're in a mad rush.'

'I bet she's been to the pictures and seen me. Or she wants milk, and we've got none to spare.'

Mrs Johnson next door was always on the scrounge for something. Being a good neighbour was a one-way business between their two houses in Flaxton Road.

But the knock sounded more impatient than Old Mother Johnson would be. The door knocker was rapped with a loud rat-a-tat-tat.

Ronnie squinted through the glass. Whoever was there was a boy no taller than he was. 'I'll see him off,' he said. He opened the door.

'Oh, my good God,' said his mother, with a cry.

It was a telegraph boy. An angel of death, as they were called. But this boy was no ordinary angel of death – it was Terry Boulter, the old mate Ronnie had met on the common the day before. He'd said he worked for the Post Office.

'Ronnie!'

'Tez.'

'Give it. Give it to me,' Ronnie's mother. She reached out her hand.

'It's not a telegram,' Terry Boulter said. 'Not the usual. It's an airgraph.'

'An airgraph? Give it here.'

Terry Boulter took it out of his leather pouch.

'No reply,' Ivy said, waving him away.

'See you,' said Terry.

'Yeah, see you, Tez.'

Ronnie shut the front door on him, and turned to see his mother leaning on the wall of the hallway, the airgraph hanging down in a fierce grip. He said nothing. They stared into each other's faces. This could have come from anyone in the services – a commanding officer or a mate, telling them how bravely or painlessly or heroically

Ronnie's dad had died.

'Open it,' said Ronnie huskily.

The airgraph was made of flimsy paper folded over and stuck down at the sides, with the delivery address on the same sheet as the message.

Ronnie watched his mother's face as she looked at the address, printed in capitals. 'It's to us,' she said.

But who was it from?

Carefully, his mother unstuck the sides, her eyes going straight to the bottom of the page. 'It's from Dad,' she said – and caught at her throat with her other hand.

'What's the date?'

Ronnie felt light-headed. Yes, it was from his dad, but the date was crucial. These airgraphs sometimes turned up years after they'd been written. It could be from some time ago, and maybe something terrible had happened to him since then. A voice from the other side...

His mother found the date. 'Two days ago,' she said. 'Sixth of May – and stamped as received today...'

Still Ronnie didn't know what to think. 'Read it, then,' was all he could tell her.

She read it aloud, her voice all over the place, with pauses and little cries, and a lot of clucking in her throat.

From 1591045 Sgt. R. Warren
At sea, HMS XXXX, Eastern waters

My dear Ivy and Ron,
A kind mate is writing this for
me on account of an ulcerated hand.
But the Americans got us out of the
Jap camp at Changi and we're on
a hospital ship home to Blighty.
All news when I see you in a couple
of weeks — God willing that you've
both come through it, too.
Cheerio for now, God Bless,

Lots of love and kisses,
R. Warren

Silence. Neither of them knew what to do. This moment had been something to dream about, but now that it was happening, things were different from what Ronnie had imagined. They didn't shout, they didn't dance, they didn't cry, they didn't kiss, they didn't hug. They just stood there, looking at the airgraph as if it was a magic light that might suddenly go out. They didn't dare to believe what Ivy Warren had just read out.

They were suddenly very matter-of-fact.

'I'll get out of this dress. I'm saving it for…'

Ronnie took over. 'Forget the pictures, eh?'

'What pictures? Get that sheet from the party. Put it in the boiler to soak…'

'Eh?'

'We'll cut that up for…'

'For what?'

She looked at him, her eyes fierce and proud. 'For a banner,' she said. 'For a bloody big banner!'

That cry of triumph Ronnie had heard before, up in Preston, from Auntie Barton. And his mind went back to Eric, who'd had his chances ruined by that Hitler-of-a-teacher called Kirkham.

'You cut the sheet,' he said.

And standing there in that hallway, thinking of

Eric, Ronnie suddenly knew what he was going to do, right now and in the future.

'Dad's coming back, so you'll be all right. I'm going to get out that letter to Matchless – and go for an apprenticeship.'

Ivy Warren looked at him, and smiled; a real smile with light in her eyes and pleasure on her lips.

'Good man, Ron,' she said.

And they threw their arms around each other and cried, and cried, and cried.

With posthumous thanks to Gunner Leonard Hudson,
who was killed on 26th August 1942, aged 26.
I have attributed his service number to
the surviving Sergeant Reg Warren.

✖✖✖

Bernard Ashley is a former head teacher
who now writes full-time. Bernard's impressive
list of titles reflects 35 years of writing realistic
fiction – from picture books to teenage novels.
Several of Bernard's books have been televised
and he has frequently appeared on prize lists –
Little Soldier was shortlisted for the Carnegie Medal
and the Guardian Prize in 2000. In addition to
his other activities, Bernard Ashley speaks
internationally on matters concerned with literacy.
He is a popular visitor to schools. His first book
for Frances Lincoln was *Angel Boy*.
Bernard lives in south London.